CAN YOU HELP ME? AND CAUGHT RED-HANDED

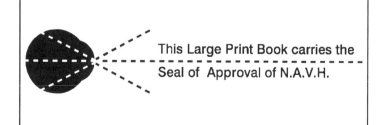

This Large Print Book carries the
Seal of Approval of N.A.V.H.

Can You Help Me? and Caught Red-Handed

TWO COUPLES FIND TOOLS FOR BUILDING ROMANCE IN A HOME IMPROVEMENT STORE

Lena Nelson Dooley and Yvonne Lehman

THORNDIKE PRESS
A part of Gale, Cengage Learning

GALE
CENGAGE Learning™

Detroit • New York • San Francisco • New Haven, Conn • Waterville, Maine • London

GALE
CENGAGE Learning

LIBRARY OF CONGRESS CATALOGING-IN-PUBLICATION DATA

Dooley, Lena Nelson.
   Can you help me? ; Caught red-handed : two couples find tools for building romance in a home improvement store / by Lena Nelson Dooley and Yvonne Lehman.
      p. cm. — (Carolina carpenter brides ; bk. 2) (Thorndike Press large print Christian fiction)
   ISBN-13: 978-1-4104-1799-2 (hardcover : alk. paper)
   ISBN-10: 1-4104-1799-9 (hardcover : alk. paper)
   1. Large type books. I. Lehman, Yvonne. Caught red-handed. II. Title.
PS3554.O5675C36 2009
813'.54—dc22   2009015346

Published in 2009 by arrangement with Barbour Publishing, Inc.

Printed in the United States of America
1 2 3 4 5 6 7 13 12 11 10 09

■ ■ ■ ■

Can You Help Me?
BY LENA NELSON DOOLEY

■ ■ ■ ■

This book is dedicated
to the members of
American Christian Fiction Writers.
The love you poured out on me at the
national conference
in 2006 was above and beyond anything
I had ever dreamed.
You are comrades in this writing walk,
and I treasure each one of you.

Special thanks to Rhonda Duke,
sales specialist
at my local home improvement store.
You helped me make my story
more authentic.

As always, this book is also dedicated to
the man who has
warmed my heart and supported me in
so many ways
for more than forty-three years —

James Allen Dooley.
I love you more than
words can express.
And I love my very own Austin,
a special grandson.

God is not unjust; he will not forget your work and
the love you have shown him as you have helped
his people and continue to help them.
HEBREWS 6:10

CHAPTER 1

Austin Hodges strode across the vast show-room of the Home & Hearth Superstore in Oak Ridge, North Carolina. He would've rather just ordered the kitchen cabinet knobs from a catalog, but the particular style his best friend Scott and his bride had chosen for their home was a special design and could be obtained only from an H&H store. Some sort of incentive to get people inside, probably so they would buy more than they planned to. If their friendship hadn't been so long-standing, Austin would've suggested that Scott and Lisa choose something else for their first home.

With fisted hands on his hips, Austin surveyed a display wall extending the entire length of one aisle. On the wall, tiny cabinet doors hung one above the other in stacks of at least a dozen, showcasing a different knob on each. There had to be hundreds, or maybe more, on the long expanse. He pulled a folded page torn from a design magazine out of his front jeans pocket and frowned at a photo the size of a picture postcard. How would he ever find the knob on the cabinets in that kitchen? He might be here all afternoon, or longer.

"Sir, can you help me?"

In his distraction, Austin didn't even consider that the question was for him until a finger gave his shoulder a poke. He turned and stared down into eyes that looked like dark pools of melted Hershey bars — his favorite snack. "Yes?"

"Can you help me?" The determined feminine face was surrounded by a cloud of golden blond hair that looked like a hurricane might have styled it. "I really need to decide which cabinets to buy, and everyone else seems to be busy."

Something about this woman intrigued him. Of course, he had never seen a blond with eyes that particular shade of brown, but it was more than that. The aura around her held an alluring magnetism, and she had a feistiness about her.

Without even folding it, Austin shoved the bit of paper back into his pocket. "How can I help you?"

The woman turned and marched toward the end of the display. He watched her quick steps until they disappeared around the wall.

In only an instant, she thrust her head back and peered at him. "Aren't you coming?" Her voice sounded commanding.

What was she — a drill sergeant? "Sure." He quickly joined her, and they headed down the next aisle.

"I'm remodeling my kitchen, and I'm trying to decide which cabinets to use." The words poured from her in a torrent. "And I'm not really sure how these things are attached to the wall. Do you screw them up or glue them?"

From the serious expression on her face, Austin knew she wasn't joking. Surely she didn't think any glue would hold a cabinet full of dishes.

"Well, ma'am" — he eyed the wooden structures they had stopped in front of — "there are several ways a cabinet can be attached to the wall. It's according to how they're constructed."

The woman stared at him with an intent expression as if she were taking in every word, but something in the depths of her eyes told him he was speaking in a language foreign to her.

"How do I find out about the ones I want?" She didn't blink as she continued to stare at his face.

Austin wasn't used to this kind of scrutiny from a woman, so he glanced back toward the displays of kitchens. "Which of these cabinets are you interested in?"

Her gaze shifted toward them before she answered. "I'm not sure — whichever ones are easiest to install."

After widening his stance and crossing his arms, he cleared his throat. "It won't matter to the guys who do the installation. They just have a basic charge for most of these cabinets."

She touched him lightly on his forearm. "I'm sorry. I must not have explained it right. I want to know which ones would be easiest for *me* to install." Then she glanced at her hand on his arm and jerked it away as if she hadn't realized she'd even touched him.

He straightened to his full height. "You want to do it yourself? Is your husband going to help you?"

The expression in her eyes hardened. "I'm not married." She spat out the words as though they tasted rancid.

Austin ran his hand around the back of his neck. "I'm sorry, ma'am. I just assumed you were, since you weren't using the installation service." After he stuffed his hands into the front pockets of his jeans, he

14

continued, "So who's going to help you?"

"I'm doing it myself, I told you." She raised her voice slightly as if he hadn't heard her the first time.

Austin stepped back. "Ma'am, let's start this conversation over. Okay?" He stuck his right hand toward her, hoping she wouldn't leave it dangling there. "I'm Austin Hodges." He waited to see if she would respond.

Several long seconds later, she gave his hand one quick, strong shake. "And I'm Valerie Bradford."

"Valerie . . . I like that." He smiled at her. "I'll feel better calling you by your name."

Finally, she laughed. "And all those 'ma'ams' were a little much. I teach at the high school, and I hear enough of them during weekdays. But at least some of the students are still being taught manners."

Austin tucked his fingers back into the front pockets of his jeans, encountering the wad of paper in one of them. Soon he'd have to get back to looking for the knobs for Lisa. "No matter which of the cabinets you choose, Valerie, I'm afraid you're probably gonna need help hanging 'em."

Valerie huffed out a sharp breath. Why did men assume that just because she was a woman, she wouldn't know how to do things? "I'm remodeling the house I inherited from my grandmother, and I've been doing all the work myself, because I can't really pay to have it done. I'm pretty handy."

As if on a mission, the man marched down the row of cabinets away from where they stood. Valerie quickly followed behind him, taking two steps to his one. She hoped the tall, ruggedly handsome stranger wouldn't get into trouble with his boss for spending too much time helping her. She tried not to notice, but his muscles filled out his blue polo shirt in a very pleasing manner. The waves in his deep auburn hair bordered on curly. One lock had fallen over the center of his strong forehead, quickly curving into the signature Superman curl. For a moment she imagined him as an auburn-haired superhero. The thought of him in tights brought a flush to her cheeks. The muscles of his legs almost stretched the dungarees to their limits, much as his shoulders and arms did the shirt. *The man must really work out. Probably has a membership at a gym. Or can people who work at Home & Hearth afford that?* As a schoolteacher, she sure couldn't.

She almost ran into him when he stopped and turned around. "Oops."

He caught her by both shoulders to keep her from crashing into him. "I wanted to show you these." He gestured toward several rows of cabinets, their doors showing through the openings in the front of the cardboard cartons. "Those cabinets you were looking at have to be ordered from the factory, but here are some you can buy and take home with you. They're a little less expensive, too. You might check to see if you like any of them."

Valerie studied the structures with a critical eye until she came to the white ones. "These would brighten up the kitchen." She glanced up at her helper. His name was Austin, wasn't it? Why didn't the man wear his name badge? *Maybe it gets caught on things or something.* She hadn't noticed whether anyone else in the store wore them or not.

Once again, the man crossed his arms. *If he shaved his head and wore a gold earring, he'd look a lot like Mr. Clean.*

"Do you need both upper and lower cabinets?"

She nodded. Did the man really think she'd replace only part of them?

"These cabinets are easier to install than the ones you order from the factory, but I still don't think you can do it by yourself.

Do you have anyone who can help you?"

Valerie rubbed her fingers across her forehead where a slight ache was trying to take hold. This was becoming more complicated than she thought it would be. "I could ask a couple of the boys from my high school speech class to help."

He didn't waver. "Have they done anything like this before?"

What is wrong with this guy? You'd think he doesn't want to make a sale. "I doubt it."

Finally, he relaxed some. "Look, I'm not trying to be difficult. If you're handy" — he gestured toward the cabinets that would go on the bottom — "you might be able to do these, but not the top ones. They're a two-man job, and at least one of the people working with them should know what he's doing."

She scowled at him, hoping he would take the hint. Did he realize what he'd said? *Two-man,* emphasis on the *man* and what *he's* doing. For a moment, anger rose within her, but that wouldn't help her, so she decided not to tell him what she thought about his terminology.

"Do you have the measurements, Valerie?"

Austin might look like a hunky movie star, but he didn't have to treat her as if she didn't have a lick of sense, as her grandmother used to say. "Yes." She dug through her shoulder bag until her fingers closed around her notebook. "Here they are."

He took the proffered notes and studied them. "Okay, you want lower cabinets all across this one wall, and two different sections of cabinets above. Is there a window above the sink?"

At least the man could decipher her drawings. "That's right."

After handing back the diagrams, she watched as Austin studied all of the cabinets in front of them. "If you use three of this model on each side of the window, you'll need seven of these other ones. You'll put the sink in the middle one. Are you gonna use the same sink or replace it?"

She stuffed the notebook back into her tote bag without taking her attention off the man standing before her. "Can't I decide later?"

He rubbed his chin with one hand. "You could, but it'll be easier to cut the correct-sized hole in the cabinet before it's installed. After it's attached, you can only get to it from one side."

"Okay." She might as well decide now. "With the new cabinets, I would like a new sink, if it's not too expensive."

Austin looked as if he was about to say

something but stopped himself. She wondered what that was all about.

With his hands thrust under the opposite armpits, he rocked back on his heels for a moment. "Look, I know you don't have any reason to trust me, but I could give you references if you want me to. I'd like to come over and help you install these, at least the top ones, but I'd like to help you with the bottom ones, too."

Valerie was surprised by his offer, but maybe he didn't understand what she'd tried to tell him before. "I can't afford to pay you much at all."

He nodded. "I know that, and we'll discuss that later. Since you're a teacher, you have weekends off, don't you?"

Now it was her turn to nod. "Of course."

Austin reached into one pocket and then another one as though searching for something. "I don't have a card with me. Do you have something to write on?"

She started to shake her head before she remembered her notebook. Once more, she pulled it from the bag. "Here."

He fished into one of his pockets and extracted a pen before scribbling something on one of the pages. "Here's my phone number. Think about it, and call me to let me know if I can help you." Austin glanced at a man walking by the end of their aisle. "Wait here. I'll get George to write these up for you and get them loaded in your truck." He loped off, leaving her staring after him.

Truck? Did he say truck? She didn't have one. Then it hit her. How was she going to get these cabinets to her house? Maybe one of the men at church could help her pick them up. She really didn't want to pay a delivery charge or have to rent a truck.

When George came down the aisle after the consultation with Austin, he was alone. For just a moment, Valerie wished the tall man had come back with him. Then a question shot into her thoughts. *Why didn't Austin write up the order himself?*

CHAPTER 2

Valerie rushed into the sanctuary just as the congregation stood to sing the first worship song. She didn't like being late, but she'd overslept for the first time in years. Spying a space at the end of a pew, she hurried toward it and slipped in. When she reached to put her purse and Bible down, she noticed the other people sharing the bench with her. A family with several children took up over half the room. With his hands held high and his eyes closed, a tall auburn-haired man standing right next to Valerie seemed lost in the music.

Austin. She didn't know he attended the same church she did. Maybe he usually went to a different service. Should she move into a different pew or stay where she was?

With a slight shrug, she faced the front and found her place in the words of the song on the screen at the front of the room. When she closed her eyes and sang along, she could forget about the man so near her . . . almost. Even without looking at him, she felt an awareness of his presence, which kept intruding on her thoughts. *Lord, I don't need to be distracted. This morning is all about You.*

At the point in the service when the worship pastor instructed the congregation to greet those around them, she turned to the people behind her. Even while she shook their hands, she couldn't forget Austin. Finally, she faced him.

"Valerie, I didn't know you went to my church." A bright smile lit his face and put a twinkle in his eyes.

"And I haven't seen you here before, either." She didn't know whether she should offer to shake his hand.

He made the decision for her by reaching toward her. When his hand encountered hers, a tingle shot up her arm.

"I usually go to the late service, but I have something to do today."

Not knowing what to say, Valerie settled on the cushioned seat with her face toward the front. When Austin also landed on the pew, he was closer to her than he had been when standing. She tried to ignore him, but by the time the service ended, she couldn't tell anyone what the pastor's main points had been. She quickly gathered her belongings and started looking for a break in the crowd that filled the aisle.

"Did you eat a good breakfast?"

At the question, she glanced up at Austin. "Did you just ask me —"

"Yes, and I sounded like my mother." A sheepish grin gave him the look of a mischievous little boy. "Sorry about that."

Valerie clutched her Bible to her chest, almost as if it were shielding her heart. "Why would you ask about breakfast?"

"Because it's too early for lunch. If you didn't have much breakfast, we could go to brunch together." The dazzling smile he flashed erased all traces of the boy. The man probably drew women like bees to honey.

"Actually, I overslept, so I only grabbed a glass of OJ."

"Good. Will you join me for brunch?"

Did she want to be one of those honeybees swarming around him? Before she could decide, an opening appeared in the crowd. She pushed into it and looked back to decline.

Unfortunately, he'd been able to exit with her, and he placed his hand on the small of her back while he bent close to her ear. "Please."

"Okay." *What could it hurt?* Since he went

to the same church, maybe it would be all right to talk to him some more about the cabinets.

Austin pulled up in front of Mother's Kitchen and Pancake House and watched Valerie fit her car into the spot beside his. She must be a good driver, because she didn't have any trouble getting into the tight space. Parking was the main problem with this restaurant, which had been here as long as he could remember. Whoever planned the parking lot hadn't had much foresight. Of course, Austin viewed everything through the eyes of a construction engineer, and he learned early on that parking was a critical issue in the mobile society of today.

By the time he exited his vehicle and pushed the LOCK button on his key fob, Valerie joined him on the sidewalk. He escorted her through the doorway and glanced around. The place didn't look too crowded. "Where would you like to sit?"

When he spoke, Valerie looked at him, and the impact of her dark eyes hit him in the solar plexus. "Anywhere is fine."

"How about over here by the window?" He urged her forward with one hand on the small of her back, noticing she seemed to be the right height for him. He could see over her head just fine, but she wasn't so short that he would have to bend too far down to — Whoa, he didn't want to go there. "The view of Oak Ridge from here is nice." After she chose one side of the booth, he dropped into the other.

A waitress quickly arrived. With a snap of her gum, she asked, "Are ya having the buffet, or do ya want to order from the menu?"

He gave Valerie a questioning glance.

"The buffet is fine." She unwrapped her silverware and arranged the utensils side by side on the napkin before looking back toward the waitress. "And I'll just have water."

"Are you sure?" Austin studied her expression. "They have good coffee. I think they even have lattes." He noticed a spark of interest that quickly vanished.

"No, I often drink water with my meals."

He gave his attention to the waitress, who stood with pad in hand. "Coffee and water for me, and water for the lady. But we'll probably have a latte to top off the meal." Before Valerie could say anything else, he stood. "Let's go see what they have today." When he offered her his hand, she took it, and he realized his mistake too late. Her touch did something to his equilibrium . . . in a way he had never experienced before.

Lord, why is this happening?

While he loaded up with scrambled eggs, bacon, and biscuits, she put small amounts of fruit on a little plate before placing a waffle on another and topping it with honey and a little granola. She returned to the booth before he did. He arrived about the time the waitress started setting Valerie's drink on the table.

"Thank you," he told the young woman when she set his coffee and water in front of his plate.

Valerie sat with her head slightly bowed and her eyes closed. He had planned to ask her if she minded his saying a blessing, but she had no way of knowing that. This one time he thanked the Lord silently, but not sharing the custom with his companion gave him a feeling of loneliness.

"So did you get the cabinets home okay?" He took a quick bite of the scrambled eggs he'd heaped with shredded cheese. When Valerie didn't answer, he glanced back at her only to find her staring out the window as if fascinated by the budding leaves on the trees.

She slowly turned back toward him. "No, I haven't worked it out yet. George said they would hold them for me until I could pick them up. I'm sure one of the men at church will help me."

Austin laid down his fork and tented his fingers over his plate. "Have you thought any more about letting me help you?"

She took a deep breath. "Are you sure you really want to do that? Don't you work on Saturdays?"

"Not usually. I pretty much have my weekends free."

"But yesterday . . ."

"Yeah, I was at H&H, but that was a special circumstance." He tried to think of a way to get her to agree. He knew she couldn't complete the project alone, and for some reason, he wanted to be the person who helped her. Maybe they could get to know each other better. He didn't realize he was staring into her eyes until she blinked and turned away.

"I could use some help, and you do go to the same church I do." He could tell from her expressive face that she was fighting an internal battle.

"Pastor Dave could give me a reference, if you want him to." For some reason, Austin desperately wanted her to agree, but he hoped he didn't sound desperate enough to scare her off.

When Valerie laughed, music poured over his soul. "I don't think that'll be necessary.

Sure, I could use your help. It'll keep me from having to ask a bunch of guys until I find one who's willing."

Their loss is my gain. "And I can pick up the cabinets for you. I have a truck."

"That would be wonderful." A relieved smile settled on her face.

"I probably need your receipt, especially if George isn't there when I pick them up."

Valerie dug in her purse, pulled out the slip of paper, and handed it to him. "When do you work again? Maybe I'll come by the store to see you."

"Oh, but I —"

"Austin!" greeted a masculine voice and a feminine voice in unison.

Valerie had watched the couple make their way across the crowded restaurant. How quickly it had filled up after she and Austin arrived. When the two did a simultaneous double take while passing the booth where Valerie and Austin sat, she almost laughed. Their movements were as synchronized as their words. Valerie wondered who they were, but evidently her dining partner knew them.

Austin rose in one fluid motion. "Terry and Sherry." He said it almost as if it were a one-word name. "I want you to meet Valerie Bradford. She goes to Word of Love, too."

When he glanced at her, Valerie gave him a questioning look. "They go to church there, too?"

He nodded. "Yeah, but they usually go to the late service." He gave a sweeping glance around the restaurant. "There doesn't seem to be anywhere else to sit. I hope you don't mind if they join us."

That suited Valerie just fine. Maybe the buffer would keep her thoughts from straying into areas they shouldn't. She had never been so fascinated by a man, and she didn't know what to think about that.

After the other couple was seated, Austin gestured for the harried waitress to stop by their table. Soon their drinks were taken care of and they also were eating plates of food from the buffet.

"It's almost like two different churches meeting at the same place." Sherry smiled at Valerie. "Terry and I occasionally go to the other service so we can get to know more of the single people in the church."

Valerie couldn't hide her surprised look. "But I thought —"

"They're twins." Austin looked as if he was trying not to laugh.

That explains the syncopation. "Twins? In-

30

teresting."

The meal proved to be a pleasant time of conversation. Valerie enjoyed watching the interplay between Austin and the other two. Even more, she was amazed by all of the ways the siblings were alike. Now that she knew their relationship, she saw other similarities. Brown hair with a hint of curl — even though Terry wore his much shorter, both of them had a visible cowlick on the left side of their forehead. Sherry cleverly disguised hers with a style that swept that direction. Their hazel eyes sparkled with life. Even though Sherry enhanced hers with mascara, Valerie could tell they both had very long eyelashes. Many of their gestures were alike. Soon they were taking bites of their food at exactly the same time, often eating the same thing. Valerie knew it was unusual for boy/girl twins to look so much alike since they were fraternal instead of identical. Being intrigued with the twins helped take her attention from the man who sat across from her . . . but not for long.

Austin studied Valerie as she discovered each new thing about Terry and Sherry. He'd known them so long they were no longer a fascination. They were just good friends, and he now knew them well enough to see the vast differences between them that weren't evident at their first meeting. When he finished eating, he leaned back in his chair and took part in the animated discussion of everything from the merits of Word of Love Church to the best place to go hiking in the Pisgah National Forest.

Not until he was in his SUV headed home did he remember that he never got a chance to tell Valerie the truth about what he did for a living. Next Saturday when he went to her house to help her install the cabinets, he needed to do that first thing. Total honesty was always best in any kind of relationship, and he had to admit to himself that he wanted a relationship with her — if it was okay with the Lord.

Valerie looked forward to Saturday more than she wanted to admit. Austin was just a guy who worked at the Home & Hearth Superstore. Of course, he did go to her church, so they might become friends, but no more. However, her heart seemed to want more.

Because they were going to work on the kitchen today, she'd eaten a cinnamon roll off a paper plate and drank her milk from a Styrofoam cup. She was throwing them in the trash when she heard his truck pull up. Actually, it sounded as though two vehicles stopped in front of her house. She hurried toward the front door.

Austin closed the door of a midnight blue SUV just as she stepped out on the porch. Home & Hearth must pay better than she realized. She turned her attention toward the large truck backed into her driveway. She couldn't read the writing on the open door because she was viewing it at an angle. The vehicle didn't have any writing on the sides as many commercial vehicles did.

"Where did you get the big truck?" With one hand, she shaded her eyes against the bright morning sunlight.

The tall auburn-haired man sauntered toward the house. "Borrowed it from a work site. Borrowed two of the workers, too. We can get this stuff unloaded faster that way."

Austin was right; with three men working together, soon all of the cartons of cabinets stood in the middle of her kitchen. Thankfully, these old houses had large rooms. Valerie had moved all of the chairs into the dining room and pushed the table against the far wall. With the merchandise, the room felt crowded for the first time in her life.

Valerie went to get her purse so she could pay the helpers. She wasn't sure how much she should give each one, but they had helped a lot. By the time she reached the front porch, the truck was pulling into the street.

"I wanted to pay them for helping."

Austin turned when he heard Valerie's comment. "They don't expect anything from you," he told her. "I took care of it."

Valerie huffed out a big breath. "You shouldn't have. You're doing enough as it is."

She pivoted and went back inside. He followed her, hoping she wasn't mad at him. When they got to the kitchen, she gave him a tour. He decided to tell her what he did later in the day, so they could enjoy their work time together. Somehow, he knew that waiting even this long to be totally honest with her might upset Valerie. It would be harder to get the work done if she was, and possibly she wouldn't want him to stay and help.

Within an hour, they had removed the old cabinets and sink. Austin had figured it would take longer, but they worked well together. Their conversation centered on the activities they enjoyed at Word of Love. Now Austin wished he had become a part of the singles' ministry. He might have met her sooner.

Valerie told him a lot about her grandmother and why she had come to live with her while she was in college. He felt that she was holding something back about that time in her life, and whatever it was had hurt her greatly. Maybe someday she would share it with him. When her grandmother died last year, Valerie inherited this house since she had taken care of the older woman for several years. He liked everything he was learning about this woman. Was she the one God intended for him? He wanted to find out.

"So, Austin, what do you like on pizza?"

Valerie stood before him with a pad and pencil in her hands. Smudges of dirt adorned both of her cheeks, which failed to diminish her beauty. Even though she had pulled her abundant blond hair into a ponytail high on her head, fluffy curls framed her face.

He stopped and took off his tool belt, laying it on one of the cabinets. "What do you like?"

A twinkle ignited in her eyes. "I asked you first."

"I haven't met a pizza I didn't like, so whatever you order will be fine with me."

She stood with the pencil poised over the paper. "All the guys in the singles' group love pepperoni, but I don't like it. How about if we order a half and half?"

Austin crossed his arms, thoroughly enjoying their bantering. "And what sissy thing will be on your half? Pineapple?"

She laughed and wrote as she talked. "Half pepperoni and half mushroom with pineapple." She raised the pencil, then made an emphatic period at the end of her sentence.

Laughter burst forth from him. He wanted to pull her into his arms.

Where did that come from? His earlier thoughts had caused a shift in his paradigm. He'd better be careful. He didn't want to move from the path of God's perfect will for his life. Maybe it was a good thing lunchtime had arrived.

"Point me toward the bathroom, and I'll wash up while you call the order in." He didn't want her to pay for his lunch, but she had insisted. Of course, a little pizza wasn't much to pay for all the labor, but he didn't want to take anything from her.

The afternoon proceeded much as the morning, and at the end of the day, all of the lower cabinets were hung. While he cleaned up the mess he'd made, Valerie ran her hands over the cabinets and her new sink, exclaiming how much she liked them. With each word, his heart expanded.

On the way home, Austin remembered that he hadn't told her the truth about who he really was. How could he have gotten so wrapped up in their interaction that he forgot to explain she had assumed the wrong thing that day at Home & Hearth? The truth had to come out, but he wanted to tell her face-to-face — not over the phone.

CHAPTER 3

Austin yawned. He'd had a hard time falling asleep last night. Working with Valerie
invigorated him in more ways than he cared
to enumerate. What was it about this woman
that seemed to burrow deep inside him? He
really didn't have time to spend ruminating
over her. After church this morning, he'd be
leaving for several days. A new project in
Fayetteville needed his oversight. He'd
probably be gone all week. Austin knew he'd
have to hustle so he could come home next
weekend. No way would he miss working in
Valerie's kitchen on Saturday.

While he dressed for church, his thoughts
jumbled together. One minute he would
concentrate on the blueprint of the building, but soon a pair of laughing brown eyes
intruded. Blond curls fell across Valerie's
forehead in the vision, and she'd swipe them
back with her forearm. How many times
had she done that yesterday? Finally, she'd

gone upstairs and tied her hair back with a bandanna. He'd teased her about the cloth belonging to her boyfriend.

A becoming blush had painted her cheeks. "I don't have a boyfriend. Why, Mr. Hodges, are you tryin' to find out more about my personal life?" Valerie had affected a strong Southern drawl that had left them both quaking with laughter.

Austin shook his head to dislodge the memory and pulled on a denim jacket. He usually dressed up more for church, but since he planned to leave after the service, he didn't want to take time to change into traveling clothes. At least no one would notice, since people wore everything from casual to what his mother called "Sunday best."

Valerie woke with a start. *What time is it?* She glanced at the clock radio on the nightstand beside her bed: 9:00. She would be late for church. After jumping from under the covers, she remembered she wasn't going to the early service. For some reason, Valerie wanted to check out the late service. Of course, she knew that a tall man with deep auburn waves would be there, too. She almost felt shameless chasing a man like that.

Well, she wasn't really chasing him. She just wanted to thank him for his help. *Right!*

Four carelessly tossed outfits later, Valerie settled on one. After putting the finishing touches on her hair and makeup, she grabbed her purse and headed for her car, finally backing out of the driveway. She would barely make it to church in time for the start of the service.

While she stepped through the open doorway from the vestibule into the sanctuary, her eyes scanned the crowded room. Not a single auburn-haired man in sight. Valerie couldn't keep her spirits from sagging. Whether Austin was here or not didn't matter. She'd come to worship the Lord, hadn't she?

Pasting a smile on her face, Valerie made her way down the aisle and slipped into the first vacant seat. It took all her effort to concentrate on the service, and she was glad she did. Pastor Dave's sermon from Hebrews 6 reminded her that God would always be pleased with the extra things she did for her students. Many of them came from families that couldn't afford much, so she used her own financial resources to give them the best education possible.

No one needed to know that even though the message lifted her spirits, heavy disappointment at not seeing Austin roosted like a vulture in her heart. When she arrived home, she wanted to avoid the kitchen. The memory of Austin's laughing face and strong arms awaited her there. After changing into jeans, a sweatshirt, and sneakers, Valerie picked up a kid's meal with burger and fries but rewarded herself with a large chocolate malt. She took the food to a nearby park and ate a solitary meal under the spreading branches of a tall elm tree.

Valerie threw the wrappers into a trash container. She walked along the paths of the park, enjoying the mostly native shrubs. Many of them were budding or in flower. Splashes of variegated greens, pinks, and whites, with a few blues and reds mixed in, provided a kaleidoscope of constantly changing shapes. Pleasant fragrances laced the gentle breeze. If anything could lift her spirits, these gardens would. *If only Austin were here to share them with me.* Valerie rejected that thought. The man probably had a girlfriend . . . or even a fiancée. Spending so much time thinking about him was only setting her up for possible hurt. She hurried toward her car, intent on preparing dynamite lesson plans.

After a week of amazingly smooth teaching

41

days and miserable nights fighting her attraction to an employee of Home & Hearth, Valerie woke early on Saturday. Since she hadn't heard from Austin all week, doubt had become her constant companion. Would he return to finish the job or not?

While she brushed her hair back and secured it into a ponytail, her ears were attuned to every sound outside her window. Finally, she heard the SUV pull into her driveway, and the vulture released its hold on her heart, which began a quick *rat-a-tat-tat* in her chest. Valerie took a deep, calming breath and skipped down the stairs. She reached the door just as the ring of the doorbell pealed through the hallway.

Should she let him know how eager she was to see him? Probably not. After slowly counting to thirty, she opened the heavy wooden door. "Austin, how good to see you." Did that sound gushy?

A slow smile spread across his face, ending with a twinkle in his gray eyes. "I've been out of town."

Her heart lightened even more. If she wasn't careful, it could float right out of her chest. "I'm glad you're back." Valerie pushed open the screen door.

Austin gestured for her to go back into the living room in front of him. One hand caught the screen door, and he closed it carefully, without letting it slam. If Gram were alive, she'd like this polite man. She could almost hear her say, *"He might be a keeper."*

His long-legged stride quickly took him to the unfinished kitchen. Austin stopped in the doorway and crossed his arms, tucking his hands into his armpits. With a tilt of his head, he studied what they had accomplished the week before. "It looks pretty good, doesn't it?"

Valerie nodded, not sure whether she was agreeing about the kitchen or the man. "Would you like me to make coffee before we start?"

"Nah, I already had some."

She liked the sound of his rich baritone voice filling her home. After rubbing her palms down her jeans, she stepped around him. "Well, we'd better get started on these."

"Okay." He followed her toward the cartons against the wall.

"Say, I —"

"I went —"

They spoke in unison, then stopped with wide grins.

"Go ahead." His gaze probed deep into hers.

"I was just going to say that I went to the second service Sunday, and I didn't see you there."

A loud laugh burst from him. Valerie couldn't imagine what was so funny.

"And I went to the early service. I thought we could worship together before I left for my out-of-town business trip." He stuffed his hands into the front pockets of his jeans. "Maybe go out for brunch again."

This time, Valerie joined in with his laughter.

The day flew by for Austin. No matter how much he tried to slow down the work, the hours wouldn't cooperate. At least they didn't get all of the upper cabinets hung. Maybe because they spent so much time laughing and sharing stories from their growing-up years. He couldn't remember ever telling a woman so much about himself.

Valerie stood across the room with her hands on her hips surveying the completed work. "Those white cabinets really brighten the room, don't they?"

Austin moved to stand beside her. Even after all the work, a faint fragrance of something flowery wafted from her. He took a deep breath. "They look good, if I do say so myself."

When she glanced up at him, her face held a serious expression. "You were so right. I never would have been able to do this by myself. Whatever was I thinking?"

"Maybe you weren't." He accompanied the comment with a quick laugh.

Without conscious thought, he reached to pick a fleck of sawdust from one of the curls that had worked out of her ponytail and now hung beside her face. That was a mistake. The strand of hair wrapped around his finger the same way being with this woman wound around his heart. He didn't want to let go, but the startled expression in her eyes told him he had better untangle it. "You had sawdust in your hair."

She wrapped the errant strand around her own finger. "Thank you . . . and thank you for all your help. Will you have time next Saturday?"

That sounded like an eternity to him. Did he dare ask her for a date? "Of course. I never leave a job unfinished." He stuck his fingers into his back pockets. "Um, I'm planning to attend the late service tomorrow. If you're going to that one, I'd like to take you out for lunch."

Valerie started gathering the small amount of trash on the floor. "That would be nice, but I should buy your lunch since you've done so much for me." She straightened and turned a questioning expression toward him.

He cleared his throat. "Actually, I was asking you for a date, and I always pay for dates."

Her mouth formed a perfect O before she bit her lip. "A date?"

"Is that a problem?" He held his breath.

She took a moment before answering. "No problem at all," came out on a whisper.

During the service, Austin tried to concentrate on the sermon. Valerie sat beside him, and even though they weren't touching, he could feel her presence. He hadn't considered that calling their lunch a date would change him so much. Since church attendance preceded lunch, the whole morning felt like a date. He'd even given Valerie a ride to church, which magnified the feeling. He hoped no one asked him anything about Pastor Dave's message.

Austin couldn't remember any woman ever tying him in knots this way. *Lord, what does it mean?*

After the last amen, Valerie reached back to pick up her purse and Bible. "That was a good sermon, wasn't it?"

Since Austin had never heard Pastor Dave

preach anything but good messages, he agreed. "Where do you want to go for lunch?"

She clutched her navy Bible close to her chest. "Since you invited me, you choose the place."

Austin wanted it to be nice, but he didn't want to overdo. "Have you tried the Italian Inn over on Creek Road?"

"No, but I've been meaning to."

Since the crowd in the aisle was thinning out, he urged her in front of him. They made it to the SUV without anyone stopping them to talk. The trip to the restaurant didn't take long, and they filled the time by continuing their discussion of their growing-up years. Austin felt as if he'd known Valerie a long time, yet everything about the relationship was new and fresh.

Because they were near the front of the line, before long the hostess seated them at a table near the windows, which looked out across a tree-lined chasm. The colors of spring spread around and below them.

They both ordered the special of the day, and Austin didn't even care what it was. He just wanted this time with Valerie.

She reached across the table and lightly touched his hand. "I've wanted to talk to you about something, Austin."

"Okay." *What is this all about?* He leaned back in his chair to listen.

"I really appreciate all you've done for me." She stared straight into his eyes. "We've gotten to know each other pretty well, and I feel I can say this to you now."

From the serious sound of her voice, he knew whatever she had to say must be important. "Fire away."

"I'm sure you're good at your job at Home & Hearth," she began.

His heart dropped into the pit of his stomach.

"But you're so talented that you could work for a builder." Putting her elbows on the table, she leaned toward him. "You might even work your way up in that business and have a better future."

Now is the time. He had hoped to be able to weave it into a conversation. He cleared his throat, trying to think of the best way to start.

"Austin!" called a familiar feminine voice from across the restaurant.

Not again!

His best friend Scott accompanied his wife toward the table. "Hey, buddy."

Austin looked around, finally noticing how much more crowded the place was than when he and Valerie had entered. Quickly, he rose from his chair and stuck out his hand toward Scott.

After shaking his hand, Scott clapped him on the shoulder. "Who's this?" He looked straight at Austin's companion.

"Valerie Bradford, this is my best friend, Scott Preston, and his wife, Lisa. I've been helping Valerie install new cabinets in her kitchen."

She shook hands with both Scott and Lisa.

"It looks pretty crowded." Lisa frowned. "I really wanted to try this place."

Good manners won out. "Why don't the two of you join us? It hasn't been long since we ordered. If that's all right with you?" He nodded toward Valerie.

"Sure."

He signaled the waitress, who was quick to take their order.

"Hey, man." Scott sounded excited. "We're going to move into the new house this week."

Lisa leaned forward. "We couldn't have done it without all your help. Thanks for getting all the things I really wanted."

That statement must have reignited Valerie's zeal. "I've been trying to tell Austin his talents are wasted working at Home & Hearth."

Thankfully, Valerie didn't see the questioning expression Scott and Lisa each shot Austin. With a barely perceptible shake of his head, he let his best friend know that he shouldn't tell her anything. Scott quickly moved his arm, probably toward Lisa's hand under the table.

"He should work for a builder," Valerie plunged on. "He might have a better future. You know, work his way up in that business."

Austin knew the moment Lisa realized what was happening. She glared at him but pressed her lips together and didn't say a word.

Oh, what a tangled web we weave . . . The words his mother often repeated while he was growing up beat a rhythm in his mind. He hadn't meant to deceive Valerie, and he hadn't actually told her a lie. He just hadn't told her the whole truth. But he wanted to be the one to explain to her, not have her hear it from someone else. And he wanted it be in private, not in front of a crowd.

CHAPTER 4

Austin didn't have a good week. He was able to finish what he needed to at the work site, and he would be able to stay in Oak Ridge several weeks when he returned. These out-of-town trips to job sites grew tedious, and the long nights in the hotel ate at his soul. Why had he been such an idiot? Why didn't he tell Valerie the whole truth when he realized she thought he worked at Home & Hearth? He couldn't come up with a good answer to either question.

Most nights, he spent a long time praying. Over and over, he rehearsed different ways to approach the subject with Valerie. The imagined scenarios always had bad endings. Perhaps he should've made time to tell her on Sunday, but when they finished having the meal and fellowship with Scott and Lisa, Austin had to leave. Or he thought he did. The Prestons even offered to take Valerie home so he wouldn't miss his flight. He wondered about the conversation in their car, but that was all in the past. What he had to do was face the future.

Finally deciding that he should wait to tell Valerie until after they finished hanging the cabinets — in case she didn't take it well — Austin made it to the airport with time to spare. He didn't want the news to upset their budding relationship. *Lord, when the time comes, please give me the right words.*

Valerie knew Austin was out of town this week. When she wasn't in class, her thoughts often revisited their times together. She had never felt about any man the way she did about Austin. Some kind of connection existed between them, but she wasn't sure exactly what it was. Of course, a girl could hope. There wasn't anything about the man she didn't like — his looks, his personality, and most important, his faith. After her background, she needed a man she could trust completely.

She spent extra time with the Lord asking Him what He wanted her to do. In all probability, she and Austin would finish hanging the cabinets this Saturday. They wouldn't have any reason to spend time together after that, but her heart didn't want to accept this fact. *What am I going to do?*

On Saturday morning, Valerie awoke early after a restless night. She usually slept later on the days she didn't have school or church — but not today. After a leisurely breakfast, she dressed. Funny how long it took for her to pick out what to wear. They were just going to work in the kitchen — anything would do. But she donned her most becoming sweatshirt because it brought out the chocolate brown of her eyes, and the flowers decorating the front made it feel festive.

When the SUV stopped in the driveway, she rushed down the stairs and opened the door. Austin glanced up at her and smiled, but something was different about him. She wasn't sure what, but he didn't seem to be as carefree as before. Maybe things hadn't gone well at work this week. She hoped Home & Hearth wasn't going to ask him to transfer to Fayetteville. The thought of not seeing him again, or even as often, made her heart react with a painful squeeze.

Austin reached for the handle of the screen. "Did you have a good week?"

Valerie gave him her most dazzling smile. "Yes, did you?"

"It was interesting, to say the least." His cryptic comment increased her feeling that something wasn't right.

Valerie and Austin worked together as a

team the way they had before. Even their easy banter returned, and they finished the job by noon. Austin started cleaning up the mess, and Valerie enjoyed the fact that their time together was extended, even if it would be for only a few more minutes. She was going to miss having him around. The man had engaged her heart. She'd tried to prevent it, because she knew their time together would end with the job.

She placed the last of the cardboard in a large trash can. "I want to thank you again for all you've done for me." She couldn't read the expression that flitted across his face. "I'd like to pay you something for your time."

Austin held up his hand as if to ward off her next words.

"I know, I know — you don't want me to pay you." His intense scrutiny made her nose itch, so she rubbed it with her forefinger. "I could make you a home-cooked meal."

He shook his head. "There's only one thing I want." He reached out and took one of her hands in both of his. "Let me take you to dinner tonight."

"But —" She hoped he didn't notice her trembling.

"I'll pick you up at seven." A twinkle lit

his eyes. "Wear something nice."

She laughed. He had no idea she had tried to do that this morning. "This sounds like another of your 'dates.' "

"It is."

Maybe she'd worried too soon. The chance of a different kind of relationship developing between them gave her all kinds of delightful ideas.

Valerie spent all afternoon trying to decide what to wear. She also gave herself a manicure and pedicure while she mulled over everything in her closet. After her shower, she took great pains styling her hair and putting on subtle makeup. Even though she had decided on an outfit three different times, she stood once again in front of the closet and questioned her choice. Uncertain whether Austin desired a more serious relationship, she tried hard not to overwhelm him. But she did want to look nice. Finally, she stepped into a slim black skirt and topped it with a rust-colored silk sweater. The outfit set off her coloring in a special way. Gold and pearl hoop earrings and a matching necklace complemented her outfit.

She cocked her head from side to side. *Not bad, if I do say so myself.*

As usual, Austin was punctual. The appreciative once-over he gave her made all of her preparations worthwhile.

Tonight, Austin wasn't driving the SUV. Instead, their chariot was a well-preserved, high-end sedan. Maybe he'd borrowed the car from someone because of their date. Valerie wouldn't spoil the evening by commenting on the vehicle.

Within fifteen minutes, Austin maneuvered the car under the porte cochere of a very upscale restaurant. This date must be important to him. She hoped he wasn't going to spend too much of his hard-earned money. A new thought entered her mind. Maybe Austin was a manager or something like that. She hoped so, but just in case, she would be careful not to order anything too expensive.

The maître d' seated them at a secluded table as Austin had requested when he made the reservation. He didn't want an audience while he told her the whole truth.

Valerie perused the menu bound in burgundy leather, then closed it. "I'm not very hungry. I just want a Cobb salad."

He knew what she was doing, so he ordered for both of them. "We'll have the prime rib, cooked medium, with the special house dressing on the salad." He remembered her telling him that prime rib was her favorite.

She opened the menu and peeked at it once more. Her eyes widened.

Austin reached across the table and took her hand. "I never invite a woman to a restaurant I can't afford."

A becoming blush stained her cheeks.

After the waiter brought them a basket containing a variety of breads and made sure they had plenty to drink, Austin finally broached the subject that had been bothering him all week.

"Valerie, I brought you here because I need to talk to you about something."

She put the whole-grain roll she'd taken from the basket on her bread plate and slipped her hands into her lap. An eager expression lit her eyes. He hoped what he had to say wouldn't dim it.

"When we first met, I know you assumed that I worked at Home & Hearth. Right?"

Her eyes narrowed, and she tilted her head. "Yes . . . don't you?"

"No."

Confusion flared in her eyes. "But you were wearing one of their shirts."

Austin shook his head. "I may have had on a shirt the same style and color, but I don't work there."

Betrayal stole across her expression.

"I was there buying knobs for Lisa's kitchen cabinets. The ones she liked best are a Home & Hearth exclusive."

Austin wanted to take Valerie in his arms. She looked as though she would need protection from what he was about to say to her. With a wary expression in her eyes, she seemed to shrink against the plush chair.

"So what do you do, Mr. Hodges?" Her brittle words sounded as if he were an ax murderer or something just as bad. She shrank even deeper into her chair.

"Actually, I own a company that constructs commercial buildings. I went to Fayetteville to oversee the start of a shopping mall there."

Instead of his words soothing her as he had hoped, her anger flared. "Just when were you planning to tell me?"

"That's what I'm doing right now." He hoped his expression conveyed how he felt.

Her spine stiffened, and she leaned forward. "And how do I know I can believe you now, since you've lied to me for so long?" Strong emotion laced the words.

"Wait a minute, Valerie." Once again, Austin held up his hand, hoping to stem the flow of her anger. "I never told you a lie. You just assumed I worked there."

"And you didn't tell me any different." She clenched her fists on the table. "Isn't that lying by omission?"

He nodded. "Yeah. Probably is, and I'm so sorry. I didn't even realize you thought that until later."

"Why would you do a thing like that?" Her brows knit into deep grooves. "I thought you were a Christian. At least, you acted like one while we were in church."

That hurt — a lot. Austin took a deep breath against the pain. "I'm more sorry than I can tell you for all this." The expression of hurt and anger on her face stabbed like a sword into his heart. "I just wanted to help you and get to know you."

"Under false pretenses?" Valerie's voice sounded shrill, but at least she wasn't raising it.

Before he could answer, the waiter approached the table with their entrées. She kept her eyes trained on her lap while the man set the plates, with a flourish, in front of them. When she glanced at the dish with the attractive display of food, revulsion painted her expression. He hoped she wouldn't get indigestion from eating it.

"Valerie . . ."

She never looked at him or acknowledged he spoke.

Finally, Austin picked up his fork and tried the steak. As usual, he could cut it with that utensil instead of needing a knife. He placed the bite in his mouth, and it seemed to swell instead of diminish while he chewed.

Valerie acted as if she were alone at the table. Instead of consuming her food, she mangled it with her fork and pushed it around the plate.

Austin couldn't think of a single thing that would salvage the evening. Finally, he signaled for the check. When he arose to pull out Valerie's chair, she got up so fast she almost turned the chair over before he could reach it. She marched out the door and toward the car with her spine as stiff as a tree trunk.

"If you don't feel comfortable riding with me, I can call you a cab."

She shook her head and waited by the passenger door. After he unlocked and opened it, she slid in and buckled her seat belt. On the ride home, Austin turned on the radio, trying to dissipate the heavy atmosphere in the vehicle. The music only added to the miasma.

How could I have been such an idiot? Valerie slammed the car door behind her and ran up the steps to her porch. She glanced over her shoulder to see Austin standing beside his open car door. The look of sorrow on his face would have affected her if the last hour hadn't happened. Now she felt crushed. Pictures from her past, with snatches of this evening interspersed, flashed through her mind like a video in fast-forward mode.

Fumbling with the key, she finally opened the lock. After entering, she leaned against the closed door, and a torrent of watery sobs released like a dam breaking in a flood. She hadn't heard the car start, so she went to the living room window and peeked out. The scene blurred through the tears pooling in her eyes. Austin still stood where he had been when she opened the door to the house, but his head was bowed.

Surely the man wasn't praying for her. How could he after all he'd done?

Valerie slumped onto the couch and clutched a pillow to her chest. Sobs poured out of her but didn't wash away any of the pain. She hadn't had many relationships. Maybe that was why she was so gullible, thinking that he cared for her. He had called it a date, but he only wanted to dump this load — weighted with his previous dishonesty — on her. A load she wasn't prepared to carry.

The man could have been honest from the beginning. If he had, would she have let him help her with the cabinets? *Probably not.* She wouldn't have a new kitchen, but was it worth the pain? *Definitely not!*

Valerie knew that no one really died of a broken heart, but how long could she live with this agony eating at her?

CHAPTER 5

Austin couldn't leave until he prayed for Valerie. Even after he got in the car and closed the door, he crossed his arms on the steering wheel and leaned his forehead against them. *Lord, please comfort Valerie and help her deal with the hurt I saw in her eyes.* When the lights — in what he assumed was her bedroom upstairs — went on, he started the car and headed home.

He paced like a caged lion all around his house, not able to settle anywhere for long. Finally, he pulled out his Bible and started reading Romans 8. Several verses jumped out at him, so he reread the words: *"But hope that is seen is no hope at all. Who hopes for what he already has? But if we hope for what we do not yet have, we wait for it patiently. . . . And we know that in all things God works for the good of those who love him, who have been called according to his purpose."*

Austin let the words sink into his spirit. "Are You trying to tell me something?" He liked to speak out loud to the Lord. "Have I been rushing ahead instead of waiting for what You planned?"

That's exactly what he'd done. He felt a special attraction to Valerie that went beyond the physical. He even thought she might be the woman God created for him. But what had he done? Sorrow filled Austin.

"Lord, I did it again. I didn't trust You and let You work things out according to Your will. If I had trusted You, I wouldn't have let the lie of omission continue."

Austin knew better. Hadn't he walked with the Lord long enough to know that he could trust Him? Especially with something as important as this?

"So what do I do now, Lord? Have I really blown it for good?"

Trust Me. The words dropped into his heart and mind.

"I know I have to trust You on this, but I really feel a need to let Valerie know how sorry I am I hurt her."

Maybe he should call her tomorrow. He listened with his spirit to see if the Lord would tell him to wait. When nothing but the peace of the Lord filled him, he knew he should apologize to her.

The last few weeks of school were always hectic, and this year was no exception. Valerie pulled into her driveway at five-thirty, thankful to be home. She had two students who needed extra help before the final tests, and she was glad to give them everything that would make them successful, even if it made her day extra long.

Each day this week and next, she planned to bring home some of her personal items from the classroom. She hadn't realized how heavy her box was until she carried it up the steps to the porch, so she set it on the nearby wrought iron table and unlocked the door. Before she went back for the extra things, she noticed the light on her answering machine blinking. She wondered who it was, but she'd listen to the message after she retrieved the supplies.

The red light was a beacon that called to her, but she took the box into the storeroom beside the kitchen. Just walking by the doorway reminded her of Austin's laughing presence for three Saturdays. Three short days that seemed like so much more. Of course, they did go out to eat a few times, too.

Her heart was divided. Attraction to the

man warred with the knowledge that she shouldn't trust him. He was too much like her father, who only said what would get him what he wanted. So many times she wanted to shout at her mother for believing the man while he manipulated her. By the time she was twelve, Valerie had vowed that she would never let a man be less than honest with her. Getting away from the hurt her father caused everyone in the house had spurred her to move to North Carolina and live with Gram.

Pushing aside those thoughts, Valerie went to the machine and punched the PLAY button.

Austin's voice filled the room as much as his memory danced through her mind. "Valerie? I guess you're not home. I'll call later."

She glanced at the counter on the machine. Four calls — were they all from him?

"Valerie? I didn't know you stayed this late at school."

Should she listen to the other calls or just erase them? They could be from someone else.

"Valerie? Maybe you had to pick something up on the way home."

His voice played through her heart, wreaking havoc with her senses. One more call. *Please, please, please don't be from him.*

"Valerie? I really want to apologize to you. I'd rather do it in person, but if this is the only way, here goes. I was an idiot not to tell you when I first realized what you thought. My thinking was muddled or I wouldn't have let it go on so long. Can you possibly find it in your heart to forgive me?"

Tears streamed down her face as she listened. He sounded so sincere, but she hadn't had any indication he wasn't being honest with her all the time they worked together or when they went out.

Her phone could be set up with caller ID. Gram hadn't needed it, but now that the phone was in her name, it was time to utilize that feature. She retrieved the directory and dialed the phone company business office and ordered the service. Valerie hoped Austin wouldn't call back until it was activated. Maybe she should let all of the calls tonight go to the machine. She could pick up during the message if it wasn't him.

The next day, one of the seniors who helped in the office stuck her head into the classroom. "Miss Bradford?"

Valerie waved her in. "It's all right, Brenda. The students are taking a practice test."

"Mrs. Jones sent you this note." The girl

placed a white envelope on Valerie's desk before going back into the hall.

After a quick scan of the room to make sure her students were still working on their papers, Valerie slit the envelope open.

"Please come to the office when you have a break," she read silently.

She wondered what the summons meant. She hoped none of the parents wanted another conference. Some of the ones last week weren't pleasant. She hated this time of year when the parents thought their children should be making better grades than they had earned.

The noon bell rang, and the students filed out. Valerie didn't have lunchroom duty today, so she headed to the office. As she approached, she saw a large, gorgeous bouquet of yellow roses — her favorite. Evidently, someone else liked them, too. For a moment, she wondered if today was Mrs. Jones's anniversary — or were the roses for someone else?

"Valerie," the school secretary said with a smile, "I almost didn't tell you to come this soon. I was enjoying your roses so much."

My roses? Why had she called them Valerie's roses?

"These came for you awhile ago. I didn't want to take them to the classroom in case you were giving a test."

"I was." Valerie stared at the large arrangement. "Who could've sent them to me?"

Mrs. Jones laughed. "Why don't you read the card and find out?" She pointed to the small envelope almost lost among the blossoms.

Valerie didn't want anyone to know just how much these flowers affected her, so she picked up the vase and carried it down the hall. The scent of roses surrounded her, making her want to press her nose into each partially opened bud. As she passed other classroom doors, some of the teachers gave her questioning looks, but she didn't stop.

She set the delivery on her desk and went back to close the door before extracting the envelope. On the way to the room, a memory had invaded her thoughts. At one point during the time she and Austin installed the cabinets, they had talked about flowers. She remembered telling him that yellow roses were her favorite. Surely they couldn't be from him, but she knew before she opened the card.

I'm so sorry, Valerie. Let these flowers convey my sincere apologies to you. I'll be calling you.

Austin

She started counting the perfect buds. Four dozen. They must have cost him a fortune. Then she realized she was thinking about Austin who worked at Home & Hearth, not the real Austin who owned a company. Tears made trails down her face, and she didn't care if she wiped them off or not.

Austin was at his wit's end. He'd sent flowers. He'd called numerous times. Yet he hadn't heard a word from Valerie. Austin still felt the need to talk to her in person, and the Lord hadn't given him a check in his spirit to tell him not to pursue this need.

He thought about going to the early service, but he didn't want to force himself on her in public. Waiting for her to pick up the phone each time he called dragged out his agony. Surely she went home sometime.

After a couple of weeks, he knew the schools were out in Oak Ridge. Of course, the teachers had several more days to finish out the year, but now those days should have ended. The schools looked deserted.

One evening, Austin drove by her house. Lights were on in several rooms, but no other cars were in the driveway, so he pulled into the next block and parked by the curb. He punched the speed-dial number for Valerie's home and waited. After four rings, the machine took over, but he didn't leave a message. Austin waited ten minutes, in case she was indisposed when he called before, then punched the number again. A repeat of the last time.

Then a thought hit him. Maybe she had caller ID and wouldn't answer his number. *Lord, what am I going to do?* Time for outside help. Austin called Pastor Dave and made an appointment with him for the next day.

"Come in." Pastor Dave urged Austin toward the conversational furniture grouping on the opposite side of his office from his large desk.

His secretary followed the men into the room and set a tray on the table in front of the two chairs. Austin would welcome the coffee but wasn't sure he needed any of the cookies brimming with nuts and chocolate chips. The chocolate made him think of Valerie's eyes.

"Thank you, Hannah." Pastor Dave poured two mugs of coffee and handed one to Austin. "You sounded serious last night. Is there a problem?"

Austin laughed. "You might say that. I'm probably the problem."

After taking a sip, the pastor set his cup

on the tray. "How's that?"

Even though Austin didn't enjoy it, he told the whole story, trying not to leave out anything. As the words poured forth, he recognized that they made him sound almost like a boy in junior high trying to show off for the girls. Wasn't that what he'd done — showed off his knowledge and abilities to Valerie? He craved her approval.

"If she has caller ID, can you blame her for not accepting your calls?" The man got right to the point.

"Not really." Austin squirmed in the comfortable chair. "What I did sounded immature while I told you the story."

"It wasn't your finest hour. That's for sure." Dave's voice held a hint of humor.

Surely he wasn't laughing at Austin, but maybe he needed to be laughed at.

"So how do you feel about this now?" Did pastors have a class at the seminary on how to ask questions? Dave always knew the right ones.

"Kind of stupid. I wish I could go back to that Saturday last month when we first met. Of course, I didn't realize then that she thought I worked at Home & Hearth. Maybe I'd like to go back to the moment I realized she thought that. If I could do it over, I'd be honorable."

"Lofty words, my friend. But don't be too hard on yourself." Dave leaned forward with his forearms on his thighs. "What is the underlying reason you want to go back?"

Austin rubbed his eyes with one hand while he thought about it. "Is this confession time?"

"Confession is good for the soul, isn't it?" A sense of expectancy emanated from the man of God.

"All right. I felt drawn to her in a way I'd never experienced before." Austin hoped that would satisfy him, but the silence lengthened. "I even thought maybe she was the one God had created for me — my helpmate."

Dave leaned back. "And you don't think that anymore?"

"I don't know. I'm still drawn to her on many levels, and I still want her to be" — he made quotation marks in the air — "the one."

"Maybe she is." A smile spread across Pastor Dave's face.

"I'll never get a chance to find out now." Austin knew he sounded discouraged, but he didn't care at this point. He needed all the help he could get.

"There's some scripture I've had to learn to live by. 'But hope that is seen is no hope at all. Who hopes for what he already has? But if we hope for what we do not yet have, we wait for it patiently.' This verse is talking about waiting on the Lord. Maybe she is the one for you, but your timing was off. You ran ahead of the Lord by manipulating your experiences with Valerie. You might have to wait on the Lord to bring it to pass."

Austin nodded. "Were you looking over my shoulder a few nights ago when I was reading in Romans? God made that section come alive in my heart. I believe you've just confirmed it. So I'm to wait on the Lord, but I can still hope. How long will that take?"

"That, my friend, is the million-dollar question. Only God knows the answer."

CHAPTER 6

Austin's gaze probed Mother's Kitchen and Pancake House trying to locate Terry and Sherry Reeves. He'd spent so much time obsessing about Valerie that he hadn't touched base with his other friends. When Terry called asking Austin to meet the two of them for lunch, he gladly accepted.

Two hands raised simultaneously in a booth across the room. Twin waves signaled the siblings' location.

After making his way between the tables, Austin slid onto the bench beside Terry. "So what's up?"

Sherry frowned at her brother. "Didn't you tell him what we wanted?"

"I guess I forgot." Terry seemed unconcerned about his lapse. He turned toward Austin. "Are you still going to help us with the seventh and eighth grade camping trip?"

"How many times have I missed it?" Austin leaned his elbows on the table. "So where are we going this year?"

An incredulous expression flushed Sherry's face. "Did you forget you offered to let us use your property in the Blue Ridge Mountains?"

Austin laughed, then turned toward Terry. "You're right. She's so gullible, she'll fall for anything."

"Oh, you two." Sherry huffed a deep sigh. "I knew you were kidding." She dug in her large purse and pulled out a notebook and pen. "We need to take care of the last-minute details."

Each day, Valerie listened for the ring that signaled Austin's persistence. When he stopped calling, loneliness became her companion. All of the times they spent together — until the last dinner — had been bright points in her weeks. Now that school was out until August, she had time to work on other improvements in the house she had inherited. Too many reminders of Gram filled each room. Even though Valerie would keep some of her grandmother's things to display around the house, she wanted to make it into a home with her own personality.

As she entered Home & Hearth to choose colors of paint, she couldn't help remembering her first encounter with Austin. Why did that man flit into her thoughts so often?

When she finished buying gallons and gallons of paint in a variety of colors and carting them to her car, exhaustion weighed Valerie down. She swung out of the parking lot and noticed the coffee shop just down the block. A mocha latte sounded good, even if she'd have to drink it by herself. She needed to unwind the knots that had developed in her muscles during her marathon shopping spree.

Valerie chose a table by the window so she could enjoy the lush foliage. She loved all the colors in the summer landscape, even the greens. She took a sip of the hot beverage and sighed.

"That sounded soulful."

She turned her attention from the window to the woman who stood beside her table. "Sherry. I haven't seen you for a while." Valerie noticed the steaming cup in her new friend's hand. "Are you with someone, or would you like to join me?"

"Why, join you, of course. We need to get better acquainted." She set her cup down and pulled out the chair across the table. "This would be an excellent opportunity. I suppose you're completely finished with school for the summer. Right?"

"Now I'm concentrating on sprucing up the house."

"That's right. Austin helped you replace kitchen cabinets. What else are you doing?" Sherry blew on the hot liquid in her cup before taking a quick sip.

Valerie fought the tug on her heart at the mention of his name. "Gram hadn't had the house painted in several years, and the colors she used were darker than I like. I'm going to paint all the rooms in lighter shades."

A bright smile lit Sherry's face. "I love to paint. How about if I help you? That'll give us time to really get to know each other. Nothing like working together on a big job to bring out every facet of our personalities."

The house was a large two-story, and help sounded like a good idea, but Valerie hadn't thought about asking anyone. "I'd appreciate it. I could make sure we have a good lunch the day or days you come over."

"I'll bring something, too."

Valerie shook her head. "I'll let you help if I feed you. I'm not taking advantage of your offer any other way."

"Sounds good to me. When do we start?" Sherry took another sip of her coffee. "Now it's cool enough to enjoy this hot brew. My brother drinks it so hot it'll scald his mouth, but I don't."

"I don't, either." Valerie tasted her latte; it was just right, so she took a bigger sip. "I'm not in a hurry. I want to get the whole house done before school starts again, but I don't plan on painting every day. And I don't have any other plans."

Sherry cocked her head as if a new thought struck her. "You're free all summer?"

"Mostly." Valerie nodded. This would be her first summer without having to help Gram, so she wanted to take it easy. She wondered where her friend was going with this conversation.

"I have an idea." Sherry dug in her shoulder tote for a pad and pen. "Terry and I are in charge of the seventh and eighth grade camping trip for the church. We drive into the Blue Ridge Mountains and camp out, instead of spending the week at a regular campground. The kids love it."

"Sounds like fun to me, too." Valerie took another sip of her latte.

A huge grin spread across Sherry's face. "I hoped you'd say that. I need another woman to help with the girls. Pastor Dave and his wife always go, too, so we'd have three women that way."

"I just love Margie. I'd like to spend more time with her." The idea was taking a strong hold of Valerie's imagination. "Being with young teens will be a change from the high school students I teach."

Sherry started scratching words into her notebook. "Then it's settled. That was easy. I was afraid I'd have a harder time getting someone else to go."

"How many others have you asked?"

"You're the first one. Woo-hoo! Wait till I tell Terry."

Valerie glanced around to see if anyone else noticed all the commotion Sherry was making. Of course, if Valerie was going to spend time with teenage girls, she'd better get used to noise. "So exactly when is this trip, and how long does it last?"

"Now she asks." Sherry lifted a page. "We'll be leaving next Sunday afternoon about 3:00 p.m. And we won't be back until Saturday afternoon."

Valerie gulped. She had thought maybe a long weekend, but this trip would take a whole week. Oh well, she did have all summer. They could start the painting job when they got back.

"What do I need to do to get ready?" *What have I gotten myself into?*

Sherry looked down at the list in front of

her. "The church bought tents several years ago. That way they could control the quality, and they're top of the line. The money the kids pay for the trip covers the food and supplies. All you'll have to bring are your personal things."

"That sounds easy enough." Valerie had never been on a long camping trip. Surely it wouldn't be much different from the times she'd gone to campgrounds when she was in the youth department herself.

"Just remember" — Sherry jotted something else down — "we won't have modern conveniences. No electricity for your blow dryer. The kids will have to dig latrines when we get where we're going. And we'll all have to pitch in with the cooking and cleaning up."

Valerie hadn't thought about that. No electricity. No bathroom. "If we don't have electricity, how do we heat the water to wash dishes?"

Without blinking, Sherry replied, "In a big iron pot over the campfire."

Having second thoughts, Valerie asked, "Is it too late to back out?"

Sherry frowned and shook her head. "We won't force you to come, but even without the modern conveniences, the camping trip is wonderful. We'll be up close and personal with nature. I've seen more varieties of rhododendrons and wild azaleas on these trips than anywhere else. And this time of year, the dogwoods and red buds will be in full bloom. Looking out across the mountains is a breathtaking sight."

Valerie began to catch Sherry's enthusiasm. *How hard could it be anyway?* "Okay, I'm still in."

"You'll need a sleeping bag. If you don't have one, I'll try to borrow one for you."

The only times Valerie had ever used a sleeping bag were when she was a lot younger. She might still have it in the attic. "I don't really think the Sleeping Beauty kind I slept in at Grams when I was little is what you're talking about, is it?"

"No." Sherry laughed. "For a minute there, I could just see you showing up with that one." She took another quick sip of her drink. "You'll need a good one. Nights get really cool up in the mountains, even in June. I'll borrow one for you. At least we won't have to carry everything in our backpacks." Sherry stared out the window. "I'm trying to remember which year it was . . . maybe three years ago. The guys picked a camping spot way up a mountain with no road to it. We lugged everything in large backpacks. I thought I wouldn't make it with my share." She turned back toward Valerie. "I told them if they wanted to camp someplace like that again, I wasn't going. They'd have to find another woman to head up working with the girls. They've been better about choosing an accessible spot since then."

Valerie was thankful she hadn't been involved with that trip. "So they're taking most of the supplies in a vehicle."

"It's the only way to camp, in my opinion." Sherry laughed. "And since they didn't want to find someone to take my place . . ."

When Valerie arrived at the church on Sunday afternoon, teens and parents swarmed the parking lot. Six large vans stood waiting as well as a pickup that had an enclosed trailer hitched to the back. Evidently, the pickup bed was fully loaded, because a tarp stretched across the top.

As soon as Valerie stepped out of her car and dragged a large cylindrical bag from the backseat, Pastor Dave came up to her. "Here, let me help you with your duffel bag." He hefted it onto his shoulder. "I like a woman who travels light."

Valerie laughed. "Well, that's not all I brought." She picked up a large zippered tote bag. "Where are we taking these?"

"I'm hoping everything will go in the trailer. It makes the ride more comfortable if we don't have to make room in the vans for any luggage." After the bags were stowed in the rapidly filling trailer, Pastor Dave turned back to Valerie. "Since you're a teacher, are you licensed to drive students on field trips?"

"The district wants all teachers to obtain that kind of license, just in case."

The pastor looked relieved. "Good. Now I don't have to try to find another person to drive. Of course, you could drive the pickup instead of one of the vans. That way you wouldn't need a special license."

"Does this mean I have to keep order in the van *and* drive?" Things were sounding less desirable by the minute.

"Actually, it's not so bad. I'll take all the more rambunctious kids in my van." He scanned the parking lot. "Most everybody is here, so we can start loading the vans. You can take the eighth grade girls. I think they'll be the least amount of trouble. They've been on the trip before, and they know the rules. The adults will stay in touch with walkie-talkies, and if there's any prob-lem, we'll all stop."

Valerie took a deep breath. "That sounds better than trying to manage a trailer behind a pickup." She looked around the parking lot, wondering which other adults were going with them.

Terry and Sherry soon had the young people rounded up and started assigning them to vans. Parents talked among themselves or leaned against their cars watching the whole circus. When all the teens were in the vans, the only people standing near them were Terry and Sherry, Pastor Dave and Margie, and Valerie. The numbers didn't add up. Seven vehicles, five drivers. *Now what?*

Pastor Dave directed Valerie to one of the vans. Before she reached the door, a car screeched up and let out two young men. They looked to Valerie as if they might be college students. One of them jumped into the cab of the pickup, and Pastor Dave pointed the other one to a van full of boys. Soon the caravan wound out of the parking lot. Valerie's van was third from the front.

"Miss Bradford?"

Valerie glanced in the rearview mirror.

At the back of the vehicle, a girl with red corkscrew curls waved her hand. "Will it bother you if we sing on the way?"

Valerie raised her voice. "Not a bit. Just don't get too loud in case someone calls me on the walkie-talkie. I want to be able to hear it."

The music started at the back of the conveyance and rolled forward. The usual youth choruses rang out, but soon the girls started singing some of the popular contemporary songs often played by KSON, the local Christian radio station. Valerie knew some of the words, but these teens knew every word.

Actually, the music was a pleasant background to the scenic route they took. Valerie's gaze often drifted toward the mountains they were driving through. Sometimes the mountains looked like the rolling waves of the ocean. Muted dark greens morphed into bursting colors as they passed through the forested slopes. The farther they went, the steeper the climb. They weren't on the Blue Ridge Parkway. Instead, the caravan snaked around twisting two-lane mountain roads.

After they had been driving for about two hours, Terry's voice called through the walkie-talkie. "A good place to stop and take a quick break is coming up on the right. Everyone let me know you hear this."

"Sherry here." She drove the lead van.

From the second vehicle came the words, "Margie here."

Valerie pushed the button. "Valerie here."

Similar responses continued down the line. Just as they finished, Valerie rounded a curve that revealed a store, complete with outdoor displays of mountain crafts and quilts. She planned to enjoy this stop.

After the "quick break" that took an hour, the trip changed. Within a couple of miles, they turned off the main highway onto a narrow, blacktopped road that eventually gave way to a well-maintained dirt road. Then it became a rough track.

Nearly an hour after leaving the fascinating store, they pulled into a large, almost flat meadow surrounded by dense woods. Valerie felt as if they had completely left civilization. Her bottom hurt from bouncing over all the bumps in the last section of road. She'd be glad to get out of the van and stretch her legs again. She hadn't realized how much she had tensed her muscles until they came to a full stop.

"You girls stay in the van until I ask Terry and Sherry what we do now." Valerie stepped down, and her foot landed on a rock and slid sideways. She pitched forward toward the hard ground.

Strong arms wrapped around her. "Be careful." The warm masculine tone overwhelmed her with memories.

Valerie looked up into the warm gray eyes

she had tried to forget. "Austin, what are you doing here?"

"I might ask you the same thing." He let her go and crossed his arms over his chest, a usual posture for him.

Valerie couldn't help noticing how his muscles bulged beneath the bright red T-shirt he wore. She had a hard time catching her breath. They must be at a higher altitude than she realized. "Sherry asked me to help with the girls."

"And I'm helping with the guys." Austin's laugh pealed across the meadow. "I guess no one thought to tell us that the other one was coming."

Valerie tried to gain some reasoning power. This was the man who hadn't been completely honest with her. She missed seeing him, but she needed to guard her heart, so she hurried around him toward where the twins stood between their respective vans. "So what do we do now?"

Sherry turned toward her. "I saw Austin help you when you got out of the van. Wasn't it nice of him to bring some of his men up here early and set up all the tents?"

How could Valerie disagree?

"He even sent a couple of the college boys he employs during the summer to help drive the vans. Some of the guys will stay around to help any way they can. One of them is even the camp cook, but we'll have to help him."

So that's where the young men had come from. "Why would he do that?" The words burst from Valerie before she could think.

"Actually, he owns this land, and he offered to let us camp here this year." Sherry's voice held such a strong note of admiration for the man that Valerie wondered if she was interested in him — maybe in a romantic way.

Why did that thought bother her? And why hadn't anyone told her he would be here? Valerie seriously wondered if she would have come on this jaunt if she had known. Maybe if he stayed with the boys and she stayed with the girls, they could keep out of each other's way. If not, this would be a very long week.

CHAPTER 7

After helping everyone settle into tents, Austin climbed one of his favorite trails. He stopped at a lookout point and sat on the flat rock shelf that jutted over the wooded valley.

"Lord, I've stopped pursuing Valerie and rested in Your care. Now here she is, and we'll be spending the week together. It's going to be hard to stay away from her, so You'll have to give me constant directions. I'll try to listen for them better than I did before." Of course, he couldn't keep from hoping she'd forgive him.

From his perch on the side of the highest peak on his inherited property, Austin let his gaze rove over the vista spread before him. He knew why this part of the Blue Ridge Mountains reminded his ancestors of the Scottish Highlands they'd left years before. A couple of years ago, he'd stood on a craggy hill in Scotland.

Taking a deep breath, Austin heaved himself to his feet and started down the steep path. A smile crept across his face, and his heart lifted. Valerie was somewhere at the end of the trail. At least he could see her for the next few days. He hoped, if nothing else, they could at least become friends again.

He arrived at the campsite and searched the area until he found her helping put together the evening meal. Hunger gnawed at his stomach, accompanied by a desire for more than just the food.

"Hey, Austin." Pastor Dave waved him over.

He jogged toward the two men who had been deep in conversation when he returned from his jaunt. "What's up, Pastor?"

His friend greeted him with a clap on the shoulder. "Terry and I were just trying to nail down the schedule for tomorrow. We were discussing whether or not we should divide the group and alternate activities. What do you think?"

Austin crossed his arms and thought about it for a moment before answering. Sounded like a good idea to him. With fewer kids to worry about at one time, the activities would go more smoothly. "I agree."

"Then it's all set." Terry marked something on his clipboard. "I'll let the women know." He trotted off toward the cooking crew.

Austin started to follow, but Pastor Dave put a hand on his arm to restrain him. "I need to ask you something. How would you feel being paired with Valerie tomorrow?"

Is he kidding? Austin tried not to sound too eager. "That would work."

Supper was a noisy affair, and Valerie used the time to try to get to know some of the girls. She wasn't sure what would transpire this week, but she would put her whole heart into it. These young people deserved her best.

After they finished eating, Terry called everyone over to an area where large logs lay arranged on the ground like seats in an amphitheater. The kids clustered in clumps with their friends, and the adults lined the back row. All but Terry.

"Here's what we're gonna do." He glanced down at the clipboard. "Tomorrow we're gonna divide into two groups. Since there are more seventh graders than eighth graders, Pastor Dave, Margie, Sherry, and I will take the larger group horseback riding in the morning. Austin and Valerie will go mountain climbing with the other kids.

Then in the afternoon, we'll switch."

Valerie took a deep breath. She couldn't remember how long it had been since she climbed a mountain. She hoped she wasn't too out of shape.

She would also be spending most of the day with Austin. How would that work? Of course, she would be in charge of the girls. She and Austin wouldn't necessarily have any interaction. *I can do this.*

Of their own volition, her eyes drifted toward the man. He was staring straight at her, and the expression on his face revealed that he hadn't been sure of her reaction to the news. Valerie gave him the best smile she could muster.

For Valerie, morning took forever to arrive. She couldn't remember how long it had been since she'd slept on the ground. Even with the thickly padded sleeping bag beneath her, the ground was far too hard. Finding a comfortable position had taken a long time, and then her thoughts had taken over and kept her awake for hours longer.

She crawled out of the tent, fully clothed. All of her friends would be surprised to hear that she'd slept in the clothing she wore yesterday. But what if one of the girls needed her during the night? If that happened, she wouldn't want to go outside in her pj's and robe.

Valerie didn't see anyone else moving around in the soft prelight of dawn. The sun hadn't risen above the mountains surrounding them, and mist shrouded the area. Everything smelled fresh and new. She stretched, trying to get the kinks out of her back. Valerie yawned and wanted her toothbrush right away, but she didn't know where to find the water to brush with. Maybe she could just use the toothpaste and spit it on the ground. After pulling her duffel bag away from the side of the tent, she rummaged inside.

Footsteps rustled the leaves behind her. She turned. Austin stood staring at her, with his hair rumpled and reddish-golden stubble dusting his cheeks and chin. For a long moment, she saw a virile man who did something to her equilibrium instead of the man she had come to know at their last encounter.

"Miss Valerie?" Shanda crawled from the opening of the tent.

Valerie looked back at her charge, but she still felt the heat of his presence as he watched for a moment longer before turning to go.

During the mountain excursion, Austin's appreciation of Valerie increased. Not only was she good with the teenage girls, but her lithe body had been created for the intense exercise. More than once, she encouraged one of the girls who lagged behind the others. Sometimes Austin wished he had chosen an easier slope for them to climb. Evidently, many of these teens never did anything more strenuous than walking around the mall. Valerie was just as good with the guys as she was with the girls. No wonder she was a teacher — probably an excellent one.

Austin heaved himself up over the ledge at the top of the trail. A small meadow spread behind him where they could rest before they started back down. That trip would be even trickier than going up. They'd really have to hold on to the trees and be careful climbing over exposed rocks so they wouldn't fall and roll down against an obstacle.

He reached over the edge and gave the girl behind him a helping hand. One by one, he pulled them each to safety, ending with Valerie. Just touching her hand shot a spark of heat all the way to his shoulder. He wondered if she felt the jolt, too, but she didn't give any indication she did.

"All right, everyone." He looked at the teens, who sprawled all around the grassy area. "Be sure to drink plenty of water while you're here. That's why we brought those canteens. With this altitude, you need to replenish your fluids before we start down."

Two boys scuffled off to the side, and one of the canteens sailed through the air and slid over the edge of the last rock they'd climbed to reach the meadow.

"Oh no!" One of the teens hurried toward the ledge. "I didn't mean to do that."

"Did you see that, Mr. Austin?" Anger painted the other boy's face red. "He threw my canteen away."

Austin started toward that boy, planning to calm him down before he helped retrieve the missing item. Before he reached the teen, a scream rent the air. He whirled to see two feet disappear over the ledge. Austin rushed to the spot. Mark, the other teen, hung a couple of feet below the top, holding on to a small tree that grew sideways from a split in the rock. His scared eyes looked like blue saucers in his pale face.

"Valerie, help me!"

The other teens crowded around.

"Everyone move over there and sit down to give Mr. Hodges room to do whatever he needs to do." Valerie's authoritative tone calmed the kids down a bit. "What do you want me to do, Austin?"

Quickly, he threw himself down on his stomach. "Sit on my legs to keep me from moving."

Without question, she complied.

"Mark, you're going to have to listen closely and do what I say."

The teen's eyes darted down toward the empty air below him.

"Don't look down!" Austin captured Mark's gaze with his. "You have to trust me. I'm gonna ask you to let go with one hand and reach out for mine." He thrust his arm down toward the teen as far as he could reach without going too far over the edge. Thankfully, it would be enough.

At his words, Mark's grip only tightened on the limb. He began quivering. So did the small tree.

"We need to do it quickly." Austin tried to convey with his eyes how important speed would be. "We don't want to stress the tree too much."

Austin didn't see how the boy could get any more scared, but the fear in his eyes intensified. "Now give me your hand. Keep a hold on the tree with your strongest one."

Slowly, one of Mark's hands released and lunged toward his leader's outstretched palm. Austin grabbed the boy's wrist. That way his grip wouldn't slip. Mark followed his example and gripped Austin's wrist.

"Good. Now let go with the other one."

The teen's attention wavered, but he quickly looked back toward Austin. "I'm really scared."

"That's okay. So am I."

Mark finally released his death grip on the tree and swung the hand toward Austin. When both wrists were firmly clutched, Austin slowly drew the boy up toward the edge. Even though the teen looked thin, Austin felt every ounce of the boy's weight on his own shoulders. When Mark was close enough, Austin slipped one arm around his body and eased him onto the grass. Valerie got up from his legs, and Austin missed her touch. They had worked together so well.

Tears filled Mark's eyes, and he swiped at them with one hand.

"Okay, everyone." Valerie's voice sounded breathless, but then it firmed. "Drink up. We'll need to start down soon, and we won't be able to use our canteens until we reach bottom. Remember, we'll have to hold on to the trees and rocks for safety."

Austin would have to remember to thank her for the distraction. He was able to talk to Mark in private.

"I was — really scared — down there." The boy's deep breaths broke up his words.

"It's okay to be afraid sometimes." Austin studied the teen's face. "I've been scared before."

"But what happened was my fault." Mark seemed to be gaining control of his emotions. "I was just being stupid — fooling around."

Austin nodded. "Yes, you were, but we all sometimes do things that aren't wise."

"When was the last time you did something stupid?" Mark's tone told Austin he believed it was a very long time ago.

"I did a very foolish and prideful thing a couple of months ago. Something I shouldn't have, because it hurt another person." He placed his arm across the teen's shoulders. "We learn from our mistakes, and I'll never do anything like that again. I'm sure you'll be more careful from now on, too."

A tremulous smile chased away the tears in Mark's eyes.

"That's why we need to keep in close contact with the Lord and let Him show us what to do." Austin almost gulped on these last words. Who was he to preach to others when he made so many mistakes himself? He sounded just like Pastor Dave.

Instead of dragging as Valerie had feared, the week galloped by. The young men who worked for Austin did a lot of the labor around the camp so the counselors could concentrate on the kids. She enjoyed every minute, except not having a hot shower every day.

Perhaps God wanted her to be here for her own good, in addition to helping with the young people. Every moment she spent with the teens and Austin helped her see how wrong she'd been about him. He was nothing like her father had been. Yes, he'd made a mistake, but she'd blown it way out of proportion. She thought she had out-grown that tendency, but God showed her that she had a long way to go before she even came close to perfection in that area of her life.

Now she wished she could figure out some way to let Austin know she wanted to pursue some kind of relationship with him. She watched him as he talked to Pastor Dave while the rest of the group packed up personal belongings. All week long, he'd demonstrated his strength of character in many ways. Why hadn't she recognized that part of him?

Austin glanced at her before turning to stride across the uneven ground toward where she zipped up her duffel. She stood and waited for him.

"I've just made arrangements with Pastor Dave for you to ride with me going back to town. I hope you don't mind." He waited for her reply.

"That's okay with me." Suddenly her heartbeat accelerated.

"I'd like to show you something before we go back." His penetrating gaze seemed to search her heart and soul.

"Sure. Whatever you want." She picked up her duffel, but he took it from her along with her tote bag and led the way to his SUV.

They drove a different direction from the camp, more around the mountain than down. On the other side, the road started a steep descent, but Austin handled the vehicle as if he were driving on flat ground.

"So where are we going?" She kept her eyes on the lush vegetation growing in the forest surrounding them, looking for the splashes of color indicating rhododendrons or their cousins, the azaleas. Their blooms were glorious in June.

The truck broke through the edge of the wooded area, and the road widened. "My ancestors settled this land generations ago. Now it belongs to me." Austin made a sharp turn onto another road. "I'm taking you to the home place."

They rounded a bend, and Valerie gasped. A lovely older home perched regally on a knoll, with grassy land spread around almost like a royal train. "That's the home place?"

The area was well maintained, and the large two-story house sparkled in the sunlight.

"Yeah. I thought it was time for us to talk." A smile lit his gray eyes and went straight to her heart.

They hadn't been driving very long. "Do you mean that a shower and other amenities were only a few minutes from camp?" She tried to look disgusted, but when he laughed, she joined him.

"It wouldn't be a camping trip if we came up to the house to bathe. But you can take a shower now, if you want."

The offer sounded inviting, but she wasn't sure she'd feel comfortable showering in his home.

When they stopped in front of the house, a motherly-looking woman wrapped in a voluminous apron came out on the porch. "Austin, I see you and the young lady have arrived. I'll have a nice lunch for you in about an hour."

He opened the door for Valerie and helped her down. "You might want to bring your duffel inside . . . if you want to clean up." He reached for the bag and brought it with them.

"Well, come on in." The woman held the door open.

"Marta, this is Valerie Bradford. Marta is my housekeeper here on the farm."

"Not that he's here very often." The older woman shook hands with Valerie. "Always traipsing all over the state working on those big buildings. And then he stays in Oak Ridge a lot of the time, too. At least I have my own family to cook for."

Austin finally convinced Valerie to make use of one of the guest rooms while he cleaned up. He wanted them both to feel comfortable when he broached the subject close to his heart.

After partaking of Marta's abundant meal, they retired to the den, where his housekeeper brought a tray with coffee and shortbread cookies.

Valerie sat on the couch with one foot up

under her. Her hair hung in damp ringlets.

"I'm sorry I didn't have a blow dryer for you." He wished he could see what those wet curls would feel like wrapped around one of his fingers.

She reached to fluff her hair.

"You look lovely." He stopped, not wanting to scare her away before he said what was on his mind.

"Not like a wet dog?"

"Never like a wet dog."

"So what did you want to talk about?" She eyed him speculatively.

Austin leaned forward, placing his elbows on his knees. "I have a confession to make." She seemed to perk up, so he continued. "I was drawn to you from the first moment I met you. And I didn't want anything to stop a relationship from developing between us."

Her eyes grew large, but she sat still.

"When I realized you thought I worked at Home & Hearth, I should've told you the truth immediately."

She nodded agreement.

"I actually tried to a couple of times, but we were interrupted. First by Terry and Sherry, then by Scott and Lisa."

Valerie seemed to ponder those words. "I remember you were starting to say something each time — so that's what it was."

"Then I decided to take things into my own hands." Austin didn't realize how hard it would be to say these words. He wanted her to respect him. "I didn't trust God to make things right and I didn't want to upset you before we finished the cabinets . . . so I deliberately held the information back."

"Why would you do that?" She sounded hurt, even now.

"Because my feelings had been growing, and I was afraid I'd lose you if you found out I hadn't been completely truthful." Here he was, a businessman who owned a company and a family farm and on whom many people depended for their livelihood, but she made him feel like a shy little boy. "I had hoped you were the woman God had prepared for me, and yet I couldn't trust Him to bring it about. I was wrong. Can you ever forgive me?"

She fiddled with the fringe on one of Marta's colorful afghans and took a moment to answer. "I have something to confess, too. I blew everything out of proportion. Yes, you made a mistake, but it wasn't that big of a deal. My only defense is that it reminded me of the hard times with my father, who was a manipulator. I lumped you with him. I shouldn't have, because you're not the same kind of man, but my past colored my feelings. God has shown me that even though I thought I had forgiven my father, I hadn't really. And that unforgiveness spilled all over you."

Hope leaped in Austin's chest. "So does that mean I'm forgiven now?"

"Yes, and yesterday in the evening worship time at camp, I truly forgave my father." Austin leaned back and rocked in the large maple chair. "I finally realized what I was doing and decided to trust God with the whole problem."

"Is that why you stopped calling?"

Did he hear disappointment in Valerie's question? "So you noticed." He chuckled. "Yes, I had to trust Him, even if a relationship with you never happened. But do you think it might work out?"

With a sweet smile, she nodded. "I hope so."

"This has been some week, hasn't it?" Austin stood and extended his hand to her. "Let's go for a walk."

Valerie wasn't walking — she was floating, or at least it felt that way. Never letting go of her hand, Austin led her out the back door and across the yard to an apple orchard. They wandered through the trees, talking about their family histories.

Finally, he stopped and turned to face her. "Valerie, I believe you're the woman God created for me. I want to marry you, but I'll give you all the time you need to get to know me better."

"Oh, I think I know you well enough to know that you're the man God created for me." She reached up and placed a quick kiss on his cheek, then became embarrassed at how forward she'd been.

Austin pulled her into his arms, and she rested her head on his chest. "Father, thank You for bringing Valerie into my life. Help me love her and cherish her the way You intend for me to. We give our future into Your hands."

When his voice died away, Valerie looked up at him and smiled with her whole heart. He lowered his face toward hers, and when their lips met, her toes curled, her world shifted, and she had to cling to him to keep from melting into a puddle.

EPILOGUE

Four months later

Austin stood at the front of the sanctuary of Word of Love Church, listening to the prelude music. Scott and Terry stood beside him. The three men watched as first Sherry, then Lisa, walked slowly down the aisle on the white runner.

The "Wedding March" pealed from the organ, and the doors at the end of the aisle opened wide. Austin had eyes for nothing except his lovely bride. Valerie had opted not to cover her face with her veil. She told him she didn't want any more secrets hidden from each other. That's what had caused their problems, and she didn't want to start their marriage hiding anything from him.

Can you help me? The first words Austin ever heard from Valerie played through his mind. Yes, he planned to help her for the rest of their lives. And she'd helped him learn to trust God more completely. Together they would forge a strong family built on that trust.

ABOUT THE AUTHOR

Lena Nelson Dooley lives in Hurst, Texas, with her husband, James, and enjoys her two daughters and her grandchildren. Aside from writing, Lena has been a speaker to women's groups and retreats and at writing seminars and conferences. Lena appreciates any opportunity to spread the gospel through mission work and writing. Visit her Web site at www.LenaNelsonDooley.com.

■ ■ ■ ■

CAUGHT
RED-HANDED
BY YVONNE LEHMAN

■ ■ ■ ■

DEDICATION

To David Lehman for sharing his
knowledge of security.
And to Michelle Cox, Debbie Presnell,
and Ann Tatlock
for taking the time to read this
and giving their invaluable input.

You are to live clean, innocent lives
as children of God in a dark world
full of crooked and perverse people.
Let your lives shine brightly before them.
Philippians 2:15 nlt

Chapter 1

Laurel Jones, with her hands around a potted plant, was leaning far into the back of her minivan when she saw the movement outside the passenger-side window.

It's just the wind moving the branches. There was no good reason for anyone to be standing back there at the burlap-balled trees next to the vinyl shed.

No *good* reason.

That thought made her freeze like she was a DVD and someone pushed the remote's PAUSE button. But she knew she had to make sure, without being obvious, whether or not someone was out there.

Neither lifting her face nor turning her head, she shot a glance through the window.

Yes. Someone stood there. She wasn't exactly in the most offensive position to cope with an attacker. Her hands eased away from the plant, and she backed out of the minivan.

Slowly straightening, she took a step back, and in her peripheral vision she saw the figure take a step forward.

She knew the gates of the fourteen-foot high chain-link fencing were closed and locked. A few managers or security personnel might still be inside the Home & Hearth Superstore, but they would be too far away to hear if she screamed.

A pickup truck was parked next to her van. *Does it belong to someone inside the store or to this person sneaking around in the dark?* The time was way past nine o'clock since she'd stayed awhile talking to her supervisor. The overcast sky didn't help, either, having turned the night into a blend of darkness and shadows.

She'd have to depend on the rush of adrenaline that provided supernatural strength she'd heard accompanied danger. Her purse, with her cell phone in it, lay right inside the back of the minivan, but it contained no weapon. The van keys were above her head in the slot on the raised back door.

What to do? Possibilities invaded her mind just as a streak of lightning lit up the sky.

Reach up and jerk the keys out? He'd be there by then, maybe even cover her hand as she reached, or he'd wrestle the keys from

120

her. Should she wait until he came near her, throw the plant at him, jump into the van, and slam down the door? She could then dive over the seat and press the LOCK button.

No, that wouldn't work. All he'd have to do is take the keys out of the slot and use the remote to unlock the doors. That would be like an invitation for him to drive her somewhere.

Maybe she could pretend not to be afraid and talk him out of whatever he had in mind.

Running wouldn't help. No one would hear or get to her in time even if she made it to the doors of the building. Anyone inside would be in an office anyway, not on the floor. To run through the vast parking lot up to the interstate might mean worse trouble. Who would stop for some girl out at night waving wildly at them?

The "who" part made her tremble.

She would simply have to use her wits, which seemed to have taken a vacation. But he was coming closer. His pace was slow, and he seemed to sway slightly. *Is he drunk?*

That could be in her favor. If he were drunk enough, she might be able to shove him. If he wasn't . . .

Pray.

Yes, pray.

Lord, help me.

Thunder sounded, and she jumped. A large drop of rain splattered on her nose.

He limped closer. She picked up a plant, ready to throw it at him if he came too close.

He stopped at the back tire. "I didn't mean to surprise you."

Trying not to sound scared, she said, "No. It was the thunder."

She set the plant right inside the van, watching his every move. He didn't move except to fold his arms in front of him. A man didn't walk around late at night dressed in dark clothing, with a brimmed cap obscuring part of his face, and stand in the shadows for no reason.

When she reached down for another plant, she saw the medical cast on his left foot. A guy in college had worn one like that after he sprained his ankle. Great! She could outrun this man. Unless he reached up and grabbed the keys. She couldn't outrun the van.

And what might he have in that boot? Duct tape? Rope? A knife? She shuddered, all her senses alert as she put one plant after another into the trunk.

"Quite a few plants you have there," he said, as if something was wrong with that.

"Yes." She felt more drops of rain. With her left hand she picked up her purse. With her right she slammed down the door. Her next move would be to snatch the keys. She'd be ready to whack him with the purse if he grabbed for her. Then she'd shove the metal cart into his legs.

"I'm . . . ," he said, and his other words were drowned out by sounds of the storm.

Thunder rumbled and lightning streaked the sky just as a cloud burst and the rain poured. When he looked toward the sky, she jerked out the keys. His hands dropped to his sides. He took a step forward. She stepped aside, ready to shove the cart if necessary.

She didn't know what he'd said after "I'm" and didn't care. She didn't want to know who or what he was or how he felt.

"Whoa," he said as the rain fell harder. "Would you mind giving me a ride around to the other side of the lot where my car's parked?"

Laurel stared, totally shocked. Something about his tone of voice sounded as friendly, serious, and polite as if he were a friend from church asking for a ride home. Her moment of sympathy quickly switched to caution. She remembered having seen a program on TV about a good-looking, intelligent serial killer who had lured young women into his car by pretending to have a broken arm.

Without answering, she sloshed around the cart, careful of her steps lest she slip in the water, soaking her shoes, or lest he run toward her, which wasn't likely unless he was faking the foot injury.

Uncertain whether the beating of her heart or the thunder was shaking the earth, she reached the front door, jerked it open, and pushed the LOCK button. She jumped into the driver's seat and slammed the door shut.

Whew! Saved by the storm.

Thank You, Lord.

She and friends had discussed what they'd do if someone tried to force their way into their vehicle. The general consensus was not to acknowledge it but take a chance to get away. Could she really just drive away if he pulled a gun? She was afraid to look but didn't think he was at the window. If she had to shove him and the cart away with the van, so be it. Maybe that's how he got the injured foot in the first place — sneaking up on women late at night.

Laurel realized she'd been operating on an unnatural calm. But she mustn't give in to nerves or weakness until she was safely out of there. Despite the shaking of her hand, the key finally connected with the slot and slid in. Now all she needed was for the engine to catch. It did.

Looking into the rearview mirror while backing cautiously, she saw the white glow of the backup lights and then the scarlet tint from the brake lights illuminating the man in black, hobbling toward the building. Holding on to the handle of the cart, he pulled it behind him.

Why is he taking the cart toward the building? The only reason she could think of was that he would be stealing the plants sitting outside the building. Maybe he wasn't a killer but a thief.

With that downpour, he'd be totally drenched. Served him right. He shouldn't have been out there scaring people in the first place.

She cautiously steered the van across the water-swamped parking lot. The *slop-slosh* sound of the wipers against the heavy rain pelting the windshield matched the beat of her heart as she headed in the direction of the interstate. Each glance in the rearview mirror revealed a figure, like a dark wavy blot silhouetted against a gray building, fading in the distance.

First thing tomorrow, upon arriving at

work, she'd report this incident.

"Of all the stupid stunts to pull."

Marc Goodson berated himself for behaving so unprofessionally. As head of security at H&H, he was supposed to be catching thieves red-handed, not hanging around outside looking like a criminal or a pervert.

He'd expected to find the guys he'd suspected of stealing lumber and had been out beside the shed, concealed by the trees, to discover whether that pickup truck was the vehicle for transporting the stolen goods from H&H. But upon seeing Laurel Jones, he'd let surprise overwhelm his good sense.

What was she doing with all those plants? He couldn't accuse her of anything until after he checked to see if she paid for them. He didn't easily become surprised and certainly never allowed some female to cause him to be tongue-tied.

When he'd tried to introduce himself, the storm had interfered. But his name probably wouldn't have meant anything to her anyway. Then he'd stupidly asked her for a ride.

By the time he reached the other side of the building, he decided not to unlock and enter through the private entrance but slogged and squished to his black sports car parked opposite the door. Feeling like a drowned rat — and a humiliated one at that — he shook himself like a wet dog, which did no good in the heavy downpour.

He managed to get into the driver's seat, his foot feeling as heavy as concrete in the cast. Trying to ignore his plight as much as possible, he slammed the door shut, found a napkin and wiped his hands with it, then took his cell phone from the inside pocket of his jacket.

Edgar Banks, his assistant who was waiting for a report, answered on the first ring.

"Just to let you know everything's all right," Marc said. He almost laughed aloud at that. "What I mean is my suspects weren't out there tonight. I'm going home."

"You'll get 'em sooner or later," Banks said. "You always do."

Maybe. Apparently the thieves were smarter than to risk losing their lives in an electrical storm. "See you tomorrow." He flipped the cover of the phone shut and returned it to his pocket.

"What's wrong with me nowadays?" he questioned aloud. First he'd broken a bone on the side of his foot when a guy had resisted arrest — decided on *fight* instead of *flight* — and he'd had to wrestle the fellow to the floor. Marc had a few sore knuckles, but the other fellow's nose would never be the same.

It wasn't often Marc had to use physical force. In fact, he was only allowed to do so in self-defense. Now, besides having a broken bone on the side of his foot, he'd misjudged the events he'd expected to occur tonight. And if Miss Jones spread the word, the thieves would know he was onto them.

Thirty minutes later, he drove his car into the garage of his grandmother's house and pushed the remote to lower the door. While it grinded shut, he eased out onto the concrete floor.

All he needed now was to slip and break his other foot. Or to get electrocuted when he switched on the garage light, because any minute the automatic one would go off and he'd be in a pickle in the darkness — much like he'd been back at the store.

After switching on the light, he found a towel and wiped the rainwater from the leather car seat. He tossed the towel aside, opened the laundry room door, and sat on the threshold to take off his shoe and set it on the concrete. Next, off came the cast. The Velcro and nylon, attached to the rubber sole, should dry overnight — once he'd wiped out the inside.

He remained seated as best he could while removing his clothing, feeling as he thought a snake might feel while shedding its skin. The process was slow, wet, and cold.

Inside the laundry room, he tossed his clothes, except for the jacket, into the washer. His once-white undershorts were dyed a navy blue hue, and he suspected the skin on his backside was the same color — the color of his mood at the moment.

When he walked into the kitchen, he saw the flashing light on the wall phone. His mood worsened when he listened to the message that said his grandmother was doing well but wouldn't be able to talk with him tonight. He missed her most when the weather was cold or stormy.

Twenty minutes later he sat on the couch in dry clothes and with one of his grandmother's afghans around his shoulders. It felt good on a night when he'd been soaked clear through to the bone. The warm bath had helped. And now hot coffee warmed his insides.

After a while he heard the signal that the washer had done its job. He'd put the clothes in the dryer later. Maybe the humming would help him sleep. He'd need something to still that feeling of having totally messed up tonight.

He switched on the TV, but another picture was playing on his mental monitor. He kept visualizing the young woman who'd recently come to work at H&H.

He'd wanted to find the right time to meet Laurel Jones for reasons that had nothing to do with the work situation. Tonight had been neither the right time nor the right way.

CHAPTER 2

Laurel had slept fitfully. One minute she felt like a victim. The next she felt like a villain.

She couldn't stop thinking about the man in the storm. Something about his voice caused her to rationalize and think that perhaps the man in black had simply been looking at the trees and really had come around to help her.

But she needed to face facts — not some obscure feeling of guilt or what-might-have-been.

To get her mind on something else, she stood on the back deck with her hands wrapped around the aromatic cup of hot coffee with its slight odor and taste of coconut creamer. After another sip of the delicious brew, she lowered the cup to the wooden railing and took in a deep breath of the fresh pine-scented morning air.

The vegetable garden looked like chocolate pudding decorated with strips of little green spinach shoots. In the flower beds around the deck, a few blossoms of pansies had been beaten to a pulp, but most of the spring shoots were intact. The boxwoods, rhododendron, and English laurel were hardy plants that could withstand not only April showers but the late May downpours like that of last night.

After breakfast she'd take the potted plants to the basement. That thought brought with it a stab of loneliness as she remembered how she and her mom used to work together with plants. Would her efforts make her mom proud?

A laugh of irony almost escaped her throat at that thought. Her mom had expected right things from her, but Laurel had never had to prove her worth. She felt a smile then. The sun shot brighter rays across the sky as it rose farther from behind the distant mountains.

"Laurel?" her dad called.

After lifting the cup for the last drop of her wake-up brew, she opened the screen door and walked into the kitchen. Her senses were further awakened by the sizzle and aroma of bacon. Her dad looked over his shoulder and smiled. "Hey, doll."

"Good morning, Dad." Laurel walked

over, put her hands on his shoulders, and leaned against his back for a moment. She thought of the many times she'd given her mom and dad a quick hug or a hasty adieu. It had never occurred to her that she might lose either of them.

"Sleep well?" he asked.

She moved to the countertop and leaned against it where she could see his face. "I had strange dreams."

He turned the bacon with tongs and put the round spatter screen over the skillet before facing her. "What about?"

"I don't remember, but they awakened me with the same kind of feelings I had at Home & Hearth last night."

"The storm?" He laid down the tongs and spread his hands in a helpless gesture. His face, beneath a bald head that only enhanced his good looks, took on a concerned expression. "Honey, why didn't you tell me you were upset last night? Just because I'm lying in bed with the TV on —"

"Dad," she interrupted, "I know I can talk to you anytime. But I didn't tell you for the very reason you'd get on your high horse and call the police or go out in the storm yourself."

"Police?" he blared before she got the entire sentence out of her mouth.

"No big deal now." She pointed to the skillet. "Better watch that bacon."

"Yeah," he said, "the pancakes, too. They're ready to be turned."

"I'll do it." Laurel walked over to the electric griddle where the pancakes had bubbled. She turned each one. "I'll tell you about it over breakfast. But only if you promise to let me handle the situation."

He grumbled while putting the bacon on a platter. "Sure, Laurel. My only daughter, who can't sleep, has nightmares because of something that happened at work, talks about calling the police, and I'm to promise to stay out of it. Now, what kind of dad would that make me?" He set the platter near the griddle.

"The kind who knows his daughter is a grown woman and can do a few things herself." She raised the edge of a pancake and saw that it was brown on the bottom and began lifting them all onto the platter.

Her dad took orange juice from the refrigerator and glasses from the cupboard, all the while muttering something about a grown woman. "Like your mom used to say, Laurel — you'll always be my baby girl."

She nodded, feeling a sudden swell of emotion. "I hope so, Daddy." She set the platter on the island and moved to a cabinet to get the bottle of maple syrup. Setting it down, she faced him. "And if this is too big for me, you'll be the first one I call."

They sat on their stools and her dad asked the blessing. Almost as soon as she opened her eyes, he said, "Now tell me about it."

Laurel did.

She let her dad rant and rave until she felt he had most of it out of his system. "Where was security?" he spouted. "What kind of place is that anyway?"

"Dad . . ." She tried to use a consoling tone. "H&H is the kind of place that gives you a discount on your building materials. It's the kind of place that gave me a part-time, temporary job. And the kind of place that sells me plants at a greatly reduced price."

He snorted, his red face turning a lighter shade of pink, which she hoped meant he had sufficiently vented. "It's the kind of place that's going to hear from me about safety."

Laurel lifted a piece of bacon onto her plate. "Dad, you promised to let me handle this."

"When did I do that?"

"When I asked if you would, you said, 'Sure.'"

"No, no," he rebutted. "That was a rhetorical answer."

"Dad, questions are rhetorical — not answers."

His eyebrows lifted, his head ducked slightly, and he gazed at her. His tone of voice grew quiet. "You're all I have, hon."

"But I'm a big girl now."

He nodded. "So was your mom."

She wished he hadn't said that. Sometimes they could talk about her mom and even laugh about a former funny experience. But other times, like this, a great loneliness welled up, threatening to bring tears.

In the light of day and feeling safe while sitting across from her dad, she wondered if she'd overreacted last night. "The man didn't really do or say anything wrong. Maybe he was a customer who left late and —"

"Laurel." Her dad's terse tone and steady gaze held a world of meaning.

She exhaled heavily. "I'll talk with security about it."

He nodded, pointing his fork at her. "And you don't leave that place alone after dark."

She promised. "If I leave after dark, I'll have security walk me out."

"And you will report this."

"Yes, Dad. As soon as I get to work."

■ ■ ■ ■

"Looks like we might have a wedding in the store." Charlie Simmons set his tray on the table and settled into the chair across from Marc in the food court.

Marc stared at the manager of the Home & Hearth Superstore. "You've got to be kidding."

"No joke," Charlie said. "Just a minute and I'll tell you about it."

Marc waited while Charlie bowed his head of brown hair intermingled with gray and said a brief thanks for the food. After his "Amen," he began unwrapping his burger. "I got a call this morning from a woman. We set up an appointment for her and her fiancé to talk with me about it." He looked pleased. "They met at the store."

Marc scoffed. "Looks to me like H&H is turning into a dating service instead of a home supply store." He removed the plastic lid from his salad, although he felt his appetite wane at the turn of the conversation.

During the three-block drive to the mall, the discussion between him and his middle-aged boss had centered around Marc's work as security agent of H&H and the considerable amount of money Marc was saving the store by not only catching shoplifters but also uncovering inside criminal activity.

"Don't knock it," Charlie said after washing down a bite of burger with a drink of his milkshake. "Those newspaper articles about couples meeting in our store keep bringing in more customers. They'll make a purchase to keep from being too obvious about looking for a mate. Some of them will end up getting married and setting up a home, and that's what our store is all about — beautifying the home. After all" — he popped a french fry into his mouth, chewed, swallowed, and then grinned — "love makes the world go 'round."

Marc could have said love also makes it fall apart. But such a statement could lead to questions Marc didn't care to answer. He gave a short laugh. "It's interesting, watching the security monitors and seeing men and women run into each other's cart or wait in the aisles until a member of the opposite sex appears."

Charlie grinned. "How do you know some of those couples aren't married to each other?"

"Easy," Marc said. "Married couples stand there and argue about wallpaper, paint, or appliances. Singles are on their best behavior, dressed up, and smiling."

Charlie wadded up his burger wrapper and tossed it onto the tray. "If I'm not being too personal, Marc, I'd say you have something against marriage."

Marc shrugged. "Never been in that state of anxiety."

"See. There you go." Charlie settled back against his chair. "At your age — what is it, twenty-nine? — you should be thinking about settling down. But you sound like a guy who's been bitten."

The snap of the plastic lid as his fingers fastened it on the remains of the salad seemed to punctuate Marc's words. "I'm in no hurry."

"Mmmm," Charlie scoffed. "So you'd rather watch customers walk the aisles of H&H Superstore than watch some pretty young woman walk down the church aisle toward you?"

Without commenting on Charlie's remark, Marc chewed on a whole-wheat cracker. He would have stopped this line of talk long before now with anyone else. But he and Charlie had hit it off from the time Marc had been interviewed for the job, and they'd both been open about their faith.

However, Marc didn't care to talk about his past private life. He drank his coffee and listened to Charlie praise the state of marriage and tell stories about his children.

Sometimes he thought Charlie was too good to be true with his reputation of being a fine Christian family man. But Marc was well aware of a public persona that could be different from one's private life. His own family had taught him that.

"Mark my words," Charlie said after finishing his milkshake. "One of these days you'll get caught." He stood and took hold of his tray.

Pushing his chair back, Marc laughed. "Charlie, you just gave another reason for *not* getting married. You referred to it as 'getting caught.' Now, who wants to live like that?"

"Anybody who falls in love," Charlie said, as if Marc should have known the answer.

Marc shook his head and dumped the remains of his lunch into the trash bin.

CHAPTER 3

Laurel had worked all morning in the basement, treating the plants that had fungus, neglect, or insect problems. She was as adamant about trying to keep plants alive and healthy as some people were about their animals. She felt they had a right to live their beautiful, productive lives and enrich the lives of others.

"Yes," she said as she watered a geranium that had only the problem of being thirsty. "Here's a nice, long drink for you. And when you're stronger, I'll find a good home for you." She smiled, remembering her mom had said plants needed talking to and touching, just like humans.

Later in the day, after having babied her plants, she arrived at H&H thirty minutes early to let Mindy, the manager of the Garden Shop, know that someone had been sneaking around outside last night and that she needed to report the incident to security.

Showing concern, Mindy advised her in much the way Laurel's dad had — not to be outside alone after dark.

Laurel agreed with that. "I should be finished by three o'clock, but in case I'm not, I wanted you to know that I'll be in the security office."

"That's fine, Laurel. Take your time. We don't want anything happening to you. You're a natural with plants." Mindy touched Laurel's arm. "For your information, head of security is called 'Deacon' behind his back. He's known for preaching morality while having somebody arrested."

Now, that sounded to Laurel like someone who'd take care of this matter properly. "Thanks," she said and smiled. She admired Mindy for having become a manager while being only a couple of years older than she. Mindy's expertise lay in the business aspect of things rather than in a great knowledge of plants.

But for now, Laurel reminded herself to concentrate on what she should say to "Deacon." So engrossed in her thoughts, she suddenly found herself in the center of the aisle and ran head-on into someone.

"Oh. I'm" — her breath caught — "sorry."

Looking up into the unusually handsome face and feeling the strength of his hands on her shoulders, she easily could have said, "I'm delighted." Something about him seemed familiar. Did she know this man? Maybe from her dreams — daydreams, that is. She could get lost in those blue, blue eyes.

Suddenly, those newspaper articles about people meeting at H&H didn't seem so ridiculous. Oh, but this good-looking man wouldn't need to go to a store to find a girl. He'd have to go somewhere to hide from the line of women chasing him.

Hoping he couldn't read her mind, she stepped back, and her gaze moved to the floor. The first thing she saw beneath the dress pants was a foot cast.

"Y — you," she could only whisper as she wrenched away from him.

"Please, wait," he implored with an outstretched hand. "You don't understand."

She was already several steps away from him when she heard the words. She was afraid she understood all too well. Seeing the manager ahead, she strode to him. "Pardon me," she said, interrupting his conversation with a customer. "This is urgent."

"Just a moment," he said to the customer and moved to a more private spot with Laurel.

"You see that man down there? Pretend you're not looking. The one wearing the foot cast?"

"Yes," the manager said.

Her breath came in short gasps. "Watch him. I don't want to be anywhere near him, and I'm on my way to tell security about him."

"What's it about?"

"He was outside in the dark last night, and now he's in here. He's either a thief or he's stalking me." She hurried away toward the security office.

"A thief or . . . stalking?" Marc could hardly believe the words he was hearing from Charlie.

Charlie grimaced. "You know why she'd say that?"

"Yes," Marc admitted, "I do." He was careful about his reputation as a responsible security agent and needed to be trusted. Never had he been accused of anything close to being a thief or a stalker.

Marc didn't think Charlie would believe that about him. But after coming to work in security two years ago, Marc was the one who uncovered a theft plot masterminded by the head of security. His own undercover work had led to his promotion. Any kind of accusation, however unfounded, could cause others to wonder if he were any more trustworthy than the former security agent.

Now, a young woman whom he suspected was the daughter of a man who had shown utmost trust in him was labeling him not only a thief, but a stalker. Marc took a deep breath and exhaled. "Can we go into your office and talk about it?"

"Sure," Charlie said. "But get that look of horror off your face. You know I trust you, Marc, and I know you have a reason for being outside after dark last night." He grinned. "What I'm finding interesting is that some woman has you riled up. She's gone to report you to security." Charlie laughed as they entered his office. "Think of the irony of that."

Marc could see the irony but not the humor. He couldn't laugh or even smile about such a thing. He sat on the couch and watched while Charlie moved to a table in the corner and filled two foam cups with coffee.

"Cream, right?" Charlie asked.

"Yes, thanks." Marc appreciated Charlie's trying to put him at ease. He handed Marc a cup and sat in a chair behind the desk. After taking a sip, Charlie set his coffee down. "Okay," he said and grinned. "What did you do to that poor girl? Are you trying one of those meet-at-the-H&H-store romance meetings?"

Marc didn't want to kid around about this situation. "You know I dislike things like that going on here, Charlie."

"So you've told me." He chuckled. "But you have to admit, she's one attractive young woman."

Marc was well aware of that even though she usually wore casual slacks and a plain shirt covered by a blue hip-length H&H smock. Today she wasn't wearing the smock. She was early. He knew she came in at 3:00 p.m. His usual hours were 9:00 a.m. to 5:00 p.m., unless he had some particular investigation going on that required him to work different hours.

Marc crossed his right leg over his left knee. He related his reason for being outside the night before. He expected to see two guys loading up that truck. Instead, he encountered Laurel.

"And a few minutes ago," he explained, "I was going to the Garden Shop to introduce myself and apologize for last night when we . . . ran into each other." He gave a short laugh. "I should say she ran into me." He pointed to his boot. "I mean, I'm forced to take it slowly, and she had a good gait.

Slammed right into me."

"Fate," Charlie said. He tilted his head and spoke as if thoughtful. "No, let me change that to . . . blessing."

"Blessing?" Marc snorted. "She's reporting me to security for being a thief and a stalker." Marc felt Charlie was enjoying the entire situation way too much.

"Then you'd better get to your office so she can report to you." Charlie's eyes held amusement.

Marc glanced at the wall clock. "Can't do that right now. I have a doctor's appointment to see if I can quit wearing this thing." He tapped his cast. "I'm anxious to get back on the exercise machines." He finished his coffee and stood. "I came in for the express reason of explaining to Miss Laurel Jones that I was outside last night because of security reasons and in here today because I work here." He tossed his cup into the trash can.

"Best wishes," Charlie said as Marc headed for the door.

Marc looked back. Was Charlie wishing him the best in regard to his foot or to the situation with Laurel Jones? Both, maybe. He sighed. "Sometimes we just have to face the . . ." *Not music.* "Verdict," he muttered and opened the door a few inches to peer out like some kind of sneak.

This was ridiculous. He wasn't afraid to approach a muscular thief twice his size and had a broken bone in his foot to prove it. Physical fear had nothing to do with this situation, however. And he understood all too well the psychological side of it. Could he never get over this feeling of having to constantly prove himself trustworthy?

Glancing around — lest she run into him again and accuse him of something else — he hobbled as well as he could out a side door and headed for his car.

Edgar Banks would likely inform Miss Jones that Marc was head of security and that's the reason he would have been outside last night and the reason he was in the store this afternoon.

Marc did manage a short laugh as he got into his car and stuck the key into the ignition. Then Miss Jones could apologize to him.

Yes, that's the way it would . . . should happen. Let her be on the defensive.

For a moment he sat grasping the steering wheel and looking straight ahead. No, he really didn't want her to be on the defensive. Last night he should have yelled out — even above the thunder and the rain and the lightning — that he was security and would protect her . . . not scare her.

This was not simply a laugh-away store matter. He didn't take kindly to being called a thief and a stalker. He could understand her jumping to conclusions, but they were the wrong ones. He'd have to set it straight. The possibility of a lawsuit — as well as his reputation — was at stake. Yes, he must apologize.

But maybe inside H&H wasn't the best place to do it. This called for an off-duty, personal call.

CHAPTER 4

Laurel could hardly believe the attitude of the short, redheaded security person who introduced himself as Edgar Banks.

After telling about her scare last night caused by the guy in the trees, she watched his facial expression change from serious to something akin to amusement. "Now, tell me again what he looked like."

"He was wearing dark clothes and had a baseball cap pulled down concealing his eyes. It was dark and stormy, so I didn't get a good look last night and I was scared. But," she said, "I saw him perfectly clearly awhile ago. He's tall and sort of . . . well, good-looking, and he was wearing a foot cast, like that man was wearing last night."

Edgar drummed his fingers on the desk. After a moment he looked across at her. "Did he try to harm you?"

"No. But he scared the daylights out of me. I didn't know what he had in mind, being out there in the dark and walking toward me."

"Did he say anything threatening?"

Laurel tried to remember. "He asked if I needed help."

"You, um . . ." Banks cleared his throat. "You found that threatening?"

Something about this man's manner was making her think she'd jumped to foolish conclusions. "At the time, yes," she said. "Something in his voice didn't sound too friendly when he asked that."

Banks avoided looking directly at her. His teeth played with his lower lip, and he smoothed his red curls . . . uselessly. They still looked unruly. The way his gaze didn't quite meet hers made her think he thought she was nuts.

He cleared his throat again. "Did he say anything else?"

"When it started pouring rain, he asked for a ride. He said his car was parked on the other side of the lot."

Edgar looked at her then and nodded thoughtfully. "You found that threatening?"

She shrugged. Edgar Banks was making her feel foolish. "I don't know. How can I say if he wanted a ride or was just trying to get into my vehicle?"

"I understand why you might have felt you

shouldn't trust him. Um, he didn't say who he was?"

She shook her head. "I think he might have, but there was a loud rumble of thunder just then and the downpour came. That's when he asked for a ride."

"So he really didn't try to harm you or say anything unseemly."

"Well, his just being out there was . . . weird."

"Why is that?"

"Out in the dark late at night?" She felt like screaming. This man didn't seem very perceptive.

"Well, Miss Jones, you were out in the dark late at night."

Laurel gasped. "I was loading plants."

Edgar nodded. "And you said there was a truck beside your vehicle. Then later he pulled the cart toward the store." His eyebrows lifted. "Maybe he had something to load, too."

That seemed possible. Amazing how another opinion could put an entirely different spin on things.

"You suppose, ma'am, you were just surprised and scared and thought the worst?"

Laurel could honestly say, "I suppose, but . . . he was in the store today and ran straight into me."

"Ran?" Edgar asked. "With a cast on his foot?" He looked at her with a tolerant expression as though he were the head of the complaint department and she was saying nothing more than why she was returning a defective item.

"Well," she hedged. "Maybe he didn't exactly run. I suppose I was thinking about what to say when I came in here and wasn't watching where I was going. But why would he be here in the store today after what happened last night?"

Edgar gave her a straightforward look. "The same thing you're doing here. Maybe he works here or maybe he's shopping. Oh." He grinned. "Maybe he's looking for romance."

"Romance?"

Laurel felt it was time for her to leave. Either Edgar wasn't very astute, or she was out of her mind and imagining things. Romance — of all things!

She thought of the dark, mysterious figure of last night. Then of the tall, serious-looking, handsome man with intense deep blue eyes she ran into this afternoon. That combination didn't spell romance to her. It spelled . . . danger.

"No offense, Miss Jones," Edgar said. "I'm

old enough to be your father. But if I were a younger man like your mystery man in the cast, I'd feel like coming to H&H with romance on my mind if I'd encountered you." He raised both palms and leaned slightly back as if warding her off lest she attack him. "Like I said, no offense. I'm a happily married man. But you seem to jump to conclusions, and I'm just trying to give you a compliment."

"Thanks," Laurel said blandly. She could have added, "No thanks," but she felt Edgar was just trying to placate her by being overly complimentary.

"And, Miss Jones . . . it's best you don't talk to anyone else here about your suspicions. You're an employee, and if you falsely accuse anyone, we could have a lawsuit on our hands." He paused, quite serious. "Have you told anyone else?"

The question rendered Laurel speechless for a moment. The impact of what Edgar Banks was saying began to register. She'd been here less than a week and was being told she could cause a lawsuit. The mystery man could claim that he was trying to meet her, or that he'd been looking at trees, then saw her loading plants and offered to help. He could say anything and she could prove nothing.

Feeling on the defensive, she said she'd only told her dad. "Oh, I did tell the Garden Shop manager."

"Mindy," he said. "How much did you tell her?"

Laurel tried to remember exactly. "I just said someone was out there last night and I needed to tell security."

"You didn't mention the cast?"

After a moment, Laurel shook her head. "No, I just said a man was out there and scared me to death. I told her about the incident quickly, wanting to come in here and report it, then get to work by three o'clock."

She followed his glance to the wall clock. The hands had neared three o'clock. She stood. "I won't say anything. But this bears looking into."

"Yes, ma'am," he said. "We have security cameras throughout the store, even outside, and after hours we have a staff security person on duty."

"Where was this person last night?"

She wondered if he was trying to cover inefficiency when he paused for a moment, then said, "Security cameras aren't as clear as we'd like during a storm."

She left the office, thinking she had no

idea why anyone would call that man "Deacon."

Walking back toward the Garden Shop, Laurel kept a keen eye on the aisles in case the man was lurking somewhere, looking for her or looking for . . . romance.

The idea!

She refused to admit that something had stirred inside her when she looked up at him and he held onto her shoulders. It was like . . . she knew him — or wanted to.

But that could be explained away, because she did know him. She knew him as the sneaky prowler of the night before.

And how in the world could she think of romance with someone who appeared to be a pervert, a thief, or a stalker? That was about as tasteful as eating cheesecake topped with boiled okra.

Tonight she'd have security walk out with her, and if that man — good-looking or not — showed up, she'd threaten to have him arrested if he approached her again.

"What?" Marc said after returning to H&H from his doctor's appointment. He'd envisioned that Edgar would have told Laurel Jones he was neither a thief nor a stalker. "Why didn't you tell her that was me and I'm security?"

Edgar got a helpless look on his face. "You said you'd be out there expecting to put an end to one of your cases, and I didn't know but that she might be part of it. I didn't want to tip your hand."

Feeling frustrated, Marc took a few steps away from Edgar, turned, and paced back toward him. "So you didn't mention that I'm security?"

"Nope. Not a word. I think I made her realize how ridiculous her charges were. But I said we'd look into it. Didn't want to chance messing up your investigation." He grinned. "Or your chances with the new employee who attracted your attention."

Marc scoffed. "You're out of your mind."

"Now, Deacon. Don't lose your religion over this. I noticed your interest the day that pretty girl started working here. Several times you've said, 'There's Firefly again.' "

"C'mon, Ed. You make it sound like I spend my days watching her."

"No, I don't mean that. I just mean you've mentioned her several times. Even given her a nickname."

"That's done around here, Ed; you know that. You're called Red instead of Ed." Marc shrugged. "It's just that Miss Jones lights up when she's talking to a customer. She talks with her hands, and the name Firefly just came to mind. She's quite animated when working with a customer. And they always buy and go away happy." He could kick himself for trying to explain himself to Edgar as if he were on trial.

Marc didn't speak aloud the thought that passed through his mind. He'd frightened Laurel twice already. How was he ever going to get this worked out? Or could he?

This didn't seem to be the day or the time for another run-in with Miss Firefly. "I'll be here a little while longer, Ed," Marc said. "I want to check some receipts."

"For your information," Ed said, "she and Mindy seem to have become quite chummy. During a break, the two of them went down to Lumber and talked to Spike, then they went to Appliances and talked to Sparky."

Marc felt he was in a dilemma. How could he convince Laurel Jones that he was an honest fellow but she should beware of becoming friends with the threesome he suspected of illegal activity? No way could he tell that to an employee.

Then a worse thought struck him. Suppose she was already mixed up with that threesome? Suppose she had been stealing plants last night?

Surely not.

No?

It happened in the best of families. He knew because it had happened in his. His dad had been a leader in the church and a respected businessman.

The business partner/accountant of Marc's dad came to Clovis Goodson, saying he had "borrowed" some money when he got in a tight spot. He didn't report everything on his taxes to make up for it, was in trouble, and asked for a chance to make it right.

Marc's dad gave him that chance. But the IRS found the discrepancy and wasn't interested in excuses. Although the partner admitted he was the one who'd done wrong, Marc's dad admitted he'd known about it and didn't report it. Being a partner and knowing of the illegal act of trying to cover up embezzled funds, Clovis Goodson lost his business, his home, his wife, many of his friends, his reputation, and his freedom for many months — all because he'd tried to be lenient with his friend.

That memory was as clear for Marc as it had been almost a decade ago. Maybe even clearer now, because then he'd experienced the ordeal emotionally. Now he could be more objective. He thought he might even be able to understand his dad's trying to protect his friend and partner.

Marc was in the business of catching thieves red-handed. But the last one in the world he'd want to catch would be the daughter of Harlan Jones.

CHAPTER 5

Laurel thought she'd have no problem remembering the nicknames of Mindy's two friends. They looked nothing alike. Mindy introduced the lanky, dark-haired fellow with spiked hair as her boyfriend. Sparky was his friend, shorter with thin light brown hair and a round face. He was stocky and muscular and appeared rather hyper the way he spoke fast and shifted from one foot to the other as though he couldn't be still.

"Maybe we could double-date," Mindy said after they returned to the Garden Shop. "Me and Spike, you and Sparky. That is, if you like him."

Like him? The guys were pleasant enough. Mindy had mentioned Laurel's scare the night before, and the guys said they'd walk her out and make sure she was okay when she left work.

She hadn't dated in a long time. In college several guys and girls had gone to ball games, movies, and other functions together as friends. She belonged to a singles' class at church, but no one really appealed to her beyond friendship.

Despite his nickname, neither did Sparky — nor Spike. During the past few years, she'd had no time to allow a serious relationship to develop. She'd been busy trying to get her education and dropping out of college for a semester to help care for her mom.

Spending those last months with her mom had helped ease the pain of losing her.

During supper break, she and Mindy ate together at the mall food court. Later, at closing time, Spike, Sparky, and Mindy walked from H&H with her. Laurel glanced around, wondering if security was watching.

About twenty minutes past 9:00 p.m., Laurel drove into the carport and saw the kitchen door open before she could exit her vehicle. She figured if she'd been a minute late, her dad would have been on the phone calling 911. Although unnecessary, his protectiveness gave her a warm feeling.

"I'm home safe and sound." She patted his arm then walked past him and was immediately engulfed by the aroma of baked cookies. A plate of them sat on the table. "Mmmm. You've been baking again."

"Your favorite — chocolate chip." He closed the door. "Sit down and tell me everything. I made a pot of coffee."

She tried to downplay the fact that the man had showed up at H&H that afternoon by first telling her dad about her conversation with Edgar Banks and his assurance that the store had both security cameras and security personnel.

However, he was livid when she relayed that she'd run into the man again. "Security is going to hear from me." His fist on the table rattled the cups and plate.

"Careful," Laurel warned. "You're going to shake the chips right out of those cookies."

"I promise you this — I'll be at that store tomorrow and I won't be waiting for that man to find me or you. I'll find him, and what I'll shake out of him won't be chocolate chips, believe you me."

She believed him.

"But, Dad," she said, "we might be making too much of this. He could be a customer who went to H&H two days in a row. We've done that."

Although he still had fire in his eyes, he was listening.

"And we've sometimes been the last ones to leave a store."

"True," he said. "And if they wanted to check us out, they could. Just like I'm going to check out this situation."

Laurel knew she couldn't change her dad's mind and wasn't sure she wanted to. What if the man had simply been caught in the rain after dark because he moved slowly? Or maybe he had bought some plants and needed to load them on a cart, like she had done. Or what if he was looking for . . . romance? Would this turn out to be something they could all laugh about later?

There they were again — those mixed feelings. No wonder that good-looking serial killer had been so terribly successful in luring young women into his car . . . if they'd had notions as foolish as she was having.

She read for a while to take her mind off the man in the cast. He returned, however, as soon as she switched off the lamp and stared up at the dark ceiling. Finally, she resorted to mouthing church songs and letting the tunes occupy her mind until she felt sleep overtaking her.

All of a sudden she was being stalked by a man in dark clothes. She was in an empty building with many hallways, doorways, and recesses. The doors were all locked. She moved into a cubbyhole, peeked around, and saw the dark figure turn down another hallway, so she ran to the next recess.

She neared the end of the hallway, where an EXIT sign hung over a door with a push bar. There was a side door between her and the exit. When she stepped out of the recess, she saw the dark figure at the end of the hallway. He began walking at a fast pace toward her.

When he was midway up the hall, the door next to her opened and someone yanked her inside. "You're safe," a voice said. "I'll drive you home."

The handsome man smiled, and his eyes looked kind. She felt safe standing close to him with his hands on her upper arms. She was ready to thank him. But she glanced down and saw the cast on his foot.

Laurel sat straight up in bed, awakening with a scream in her throat.

What was going on?

After many deep breaths, she settled back on her pillows. Maybe dreams didn't always mean anything, but she knew this one occurred because of the fright she'd had that dark, stormy night. But why that feeling of being safe and then discovering her rescuer was her stalker? Or . . . her stalker was her rescuer?

■ ■ ■ ■

Later that morning, Laurel did what she loved most, which was help her dad's landscaper work at his new development that he'd bought after her mom died. He'd gone from being a builder to a developer but still helped out with the carpentry at times.

So did she.

He'd taught her at an early age how to drive a nail into a thick board with only a couple of whacks. Her love, however, was not just planning a landscape but helping it materialize. She'd worked for several hours during the morning, raking and picking up rocks and throwing them into a pile, and wheelbarrowing roots and debris, all the while thinking the workers could be neater with pieces of wood and nails.

She returned home to eat lunch and take a shower before going to work. Realizing she could use a good manicure but lacked the time, she applied lotion to her hands and massaged it into her palms, which were still red from the morning's work, despite the fact that she'd worn gloves.

All of a sudden she stopped rubbing in the lotion. Her breath caught as a memory of another time when her palms were red began to trickle into her consciousness. That was like a lifetime ago. Well, she supposed it really had been. It was before her mom became ill. Before she died. Before Laurel even knew tragedies and suffering could touch her life. That had been childhood, an ideal existence.

Her mind traveled back in time to when she was thirteen. Her mom had taken Laurel and her friend Katie to a development where a house was being built. While her mom talked to the buyer of the house about interior design and paint colors, Laurel and Katie decided to inspect the premises.

Going around to the back of the house, Laurel had almost run into a piece of discarded wire mesh, the kind workers put down on gravel driveways before pouring concrete. To dodge it, she tripped over a piece of wood, fell face forward into a mound of dirt and rocks, and caught herself with her hands.

She sat up, ready to cry. She stared at her hands, red from the fall and from the mud. Before she knew it, a carpenter laid down his hammer and rushed over to her. "Here. I know what to do about that. Come over to the spigot."

He had gorgeous blue eyes and a nice

voice. He turned on the faucet and led her hand under the water. "My mother always did this for me when I got hurt. She'd say the water would wash the hurt down the drain."

Not only the water, but the gentle, caring sound of his voice eased the pain.

After the water had washed away the mud, he said, "Let me see." He held her wrists gently as she stretched out her hands for his inspection.

He'd stared at her hands, pink from the fall but otherwise not damaged. "Hmmm. I think you'll live."

She wasn't supposed to be too friendly with workers or men she didn't know. She simply stared into his smiling eyes, not knowing what to say. She couldn't remember any man ever having touched her except her dad.

He stood. "Be careful." He went back inside the frame of the house and began pounding a nail into a board, seemingly oblivious to her and Katie.

She told her mother about it at the site. Later during supper, they mentioned it to her dad. Laurel had been afraid her dad might be angry that the man had held her hand under the water and helped her, since she'd been warned about safety measures.

Her parents assured her that it was all right, that some men were kind but sometimes it was hard to judge that.

"What's his name?" Laurel had asked.

"A worker," her dad replied.

Laurel asked how old he was, and her dad sort of barked that the worker was out of his teens.

"I didn't say thank you," she told her parents.

"He told me about it," her dad said. "I thanked him for you."

For the rest of that summer she had a crush on "that curly-haired older man." A couple of other times her mom took her and Katie to the development. When they saw him, they'd giggle. Since Laurel didn't know his name, she thought of him as her carpenter.

Then it seemed her mother had all kinds of projects for her to help with and plans for her summer. Almost before she knew it, August came. She returned to school.

She forgot about the incident until a few years later. She'd been washing out a glass in the sink. When she shoved the dishcloth into it and turned it, the fragile glass broke and cut her hand.

Her mom had rushed to her and told her to wash the soap off with clear water. "Let the hurt wash down the drain," she'd said.

Being a teenager, Laurel had balked, remembering the incident with the man at the work site. "Moooom, I'm not a child."

"No," her mom agreed, holding Laurel's hand under the stream of clear water. "But it's a nice phrase, isn't it? And I know this hurts." Her mom wrapped a clean towel around Laurel's hand.

What hurt was the fact that her mother remembered what Laurel had told her years before, which seemed to be an invasion into Laurel's private memory of her special carpenter. That had been her very first crush on an older man who looked like a movie star.

Now that she thought of it, that had been her only crush on such a man.

Laurel remembered those words of advice again a couple of years ago, when her mother was terminally ill, then again after her death. Laurel had stood in the shower crying and praying the hurt would wash away, down the drain. Only time had eased the grief and the pain of missing her mom.

Why did she think of that now?

She touched her left wrist with her right hand and remembered the man's caring touch, his gentle voice, his blue, blue eyes in a suntanned face surrounded by unruly dark curls.

Suddenly, she knew.

This man — whatever he was . . . thief, stalker — reminded her of her first teenage crush. Young she had been, but the feelings had not been trivial.

Her villain's face wasn't sunburned, nor was his dark hair unruly. But his voice held a mesmerizing quality. And his eyes were Carolina sky blue.

Was it possible that the stalker could be . . . her carpenter?

CHAPTER 6

Marc got out of his sports car and hobbled toward the house where workers were on the roof, putting on gray tiles. He recognized the stance of Harlan Jones, straddling the roof with his hands on his waist.

Jones apparently saw Marc, judging from the way he hurried down the roof, scampered down the ladder, and dodged around building materials on the ground.

Marc wondered what kind of reception he'd get from this man who had been like a dad to him one summer — and a friend after that. He was finding his answer as Harlan looked at the cast, then lifted his gaze to Marc's face. The look in his eyes resembled the surprised and suspicious look Marc had seen in the eyes of Laurel Jones.

Harlan offered no welcoming hug.

"Sir, could we go somewhere and talk?" Marc asked.

"You bet," came Harlan Jones's quick

answer almost before Marc finished asking the question.

The absence of a warm greeting from Harlan told Marc all he needed to know about the relationship between this man and Laurel Jones. She was still his young daughter who had walked in the development where he worked one summer so long ago.

Harlan's long strides led him to the front of the house, where he picked up one of several boards that were on the ground and laid it on the frame for steps.

Marc wasn't sure he should take a seat beside Harlan, but the man gestured for him to sit. Marc did, but he missed the smile and hug from this man who'd befriended him one summer when he'd needed it most.

"Been awhile," Harlan said stiffly.

"Over two years." Marc was wondering how to broach the topic he'd come to discuss. Harlan probably was wondering the same thing, judging from his flushed face, which Marc suspected had something to do with a fellow in a foot cast who had scared his daughter.

"How's the police business in Charlotte?" Harlan snapped.

Marc felt Harlan's eyes boring into his, reminding him of the way the electric drill lying behind them could bore a hole through

173

a two-by-four lickety-split.

"I'm not on the force anymore."

"What're you doing?"

"Something more secretive," Marc said. "Instead of confronting criminals outright, I have to figure out who's doing what — when and how. Sometimes it gets to be a sneaky business."

"Detective?"

"In a sense. I'm head of security at a store out in west Oak Ridge."

"Security?" Harlan's word came slowly, as though he might be onto something. "What store?"

Marc stuck his booted foot out in front of him and turned his head toward Harlan. "Home & Hearth Superstore."

The crease that had knitted Harlan's brows together began to smooth out. Speculation replaced the questioning in his eyes, and a look of irony settled on his face. His gaze flitted to the cast and back to Marc's face. A trace of a grin touched his lips. "So you're the man Laurel saw prowling around outside the store after dark."

Marc nodded. "I know that's what it looked like, but I was out there expecting to catch a couple of guys I've suspected of stealing from the store."

Harlan's brow wrinkled. "If you know,

can't you arrest them?"

"It's simpler if I catch them in the act — red-handed, so to speak. I want enough evidence without having a court case or chancing the store being sued." Marc gave a short laugh. "Not good for business."

"Laurel says you approached her twice. Why didn't you simply tell Laurel who you are?"

Approach wasn't exactly the right word. Marc took a moment to think of how to say it tactfully. "First," he said, "I was surprised to see Laurel. I knew she was about the age of your daughter, but Laurel was just a kid the last time I saw her. I don't think my name would mean anything to her."

Harlan nodded his understanding.

"But even if she were your daughter, she's still an employee. I couldn't just blurt out that I was outside trying to catch a thief. Sorry to say this, but I didn't know if she was stealing the plants . . . or what."

Harlan reared back. "You thought Laurel was a thief?"

"No. Yes. I mean . . . I didn't know."

Harlan began to laugh.

Marc stared at him, uncertain whether his laughter was a prelude to something more threatening.

Finally, Harlan stopped laughing. "That's

what she thought about you." He cleared his throat. "Sorry. I can see you don't think this is funny."

"No, sir," Marc replied immediately. "I was on my way to introduce myself and apologize for scaring her the night of the storm when she ran right into me. Then she ran from me. She reported me to the manager and my assistant as a thief and a stalker."

Rearing back, Harlan asked, "Is that causing a problem for you?"

"Not with the manager and my assistant." He glanced at Harlan. "The manager is a fine Christian man, and we've become friends. He knows my family history and, like you, doesn't blame me."

Harlan nodded. "Good."

"And my assistant didn't want to tell Laurel anything that might hamper my investigation. You see, Laurel's supervisor is under suspicion simply because she's a friend of two guys I suspect. That's not the kind of thing I can tell Laurel, her being an employee. She and her supervisor seem to get along great."

"Can you tell me what you suspect the two guys of?"

"Sure. The receipts aren't matching up with some missing material. A couple of builders have come in and bought new appliances, saying theirs were stolen."

Harlan was nodding. "I thought it might be something like that. I'm a developer now, but we builders used to confide in each other about materials being stolen from our work projects. A lot of times we had reasons to suspect some of our workers or store personnel."

"Let me assure you," Marc said, "most all the personnel at H&H are honest. But there are always those few who cause trouble. A store like that is a perfect setup for criminal activity. A builder comes in and buys materials and the workers know where it's to be delivered. All they need is a pickup truck and a dark night and a house in a secluded area. I can't go to the site, since I'm not a police officer anymore. I have to catch those on the grounds who are stealing. And I can't accuse without evidence."

"I see your dilemma," Harlan said. "That might explain why your assistant didn't tell Laurel who you were and implied you might be looking for romance."

Marc gasped. "He never should have said that."

"Are you married?"

"No."

"Spoken for?"

"No."

"But you're not looking for romance?"

"Well . . ." Marc was at a loss for words. Finally, he found some. "I'm not the kind of guy to walk the aisles of the store looking for it — like those couples in the newspaper articles."

"She's not a kid anymore, you know."

Marc turned his head away for a moment, lest this man read on his face or in his eyes that he was well aware of that fact. "She doesn't trust me, and she's run from me twice. I . . . um . . . don't suppose you could put in a good word for me?"

"Nope," Harlan said.

Turning his head quickly, Marc stared at Harlan, who grinned. "That's your job. But maybe I can help you out a little."

Marc stood when Harlan did.

"We got off on the wrong foot when you walked up here," Harlan said. "Pun intended." He spread his arms. "Now let's have a proper greeting."

When Harlan hugged him tight and slapped his shoulders, Marc felt like it was old times. He was still in the good graces of this man, whom he admired more than anyone.

When Harlan stepped back, Marc thought the big man wiped at a tear. "Come to supper tonight," he said. "I grill a mean steak. You remember where I live?"

Oak Ridge Estates wasn't an easy area to forget. "Same place?"

"Yes. It's like Carolyn is all over the place. I'm not ready to leave it."

Marc saw the look of loss on his face. He hadn't known of Harlan's wife's illness until it was all over. On one of his visits from Charlotte, he'd stopped by a site. The two of them had gone to Harlan's house and talked about it.

Marc had called Harlan when he'd returned to Oak Ridge two years ago and discovered he'd gone to Europe with his daughter for the summer. Having been busy with his grandmother's affairs, Marc hadn't tried to contact him again.

"It's Laurel's day off," Harlan said. He turned and picked up the electric drill from the porch. "We usually eat around six. Come early, if you like." He nodded toward the step.

Marc straightened the step and Harlan opened a box of screws. Marc held the board in place. The years seemed to fade away. Marc welcomed the whine of the drill, the metallic odor, and the wisps of sawdust as the nails went into the wood. Marc picked up one board after another, and with the two of them working together, all of the steps were attached in no time flat.

Harlan Jones was a developer now, he'd said. Years ago, he'd been a builder. Marc knew he'd always think of Harlan Jones as being a developer and builder of a young man named Marc Goodson, who almost a decade ago had needed someone to show faith and trust in him.

Hearing footsteps on the back deck, Laurel looked up from her crouched position and loosened her grip on a pot of black-eyed Susans. The first thing she saw through the railings were three tennis shoes and a foot cast.

The shock of it sent the Susans rolling down the slight incline and her careening to her backside. She barely caught herself before rolling down the hill herself.

This had to be a dream. There she was, in shorts and a grimy T-shirt — not to mention dirty, sweaty skin and hair wet from the sun's rays. No way could this be reality, because that would mean she'd been frightened twice by the same man while she held a potted plant in her hands.

The stalker had a grimace on his handsome face and a look of uncertainty in his blue eyes. He didn't move, but her dad walked to the railing and looked over. "You all right, Laurel?"

She gave him her best "whadda ya think?" look. Did he think she always fell on her backside while a pot of flowers rolled down the hill?

While her dad chuckled, she was thinking there were several options here.

One, she was having a nightmare.

Two, the stalker had found out where they lived and was holding her dad at gunpoint to get to her.

Three, her dad had tracked down the stalker and was going to kill him right before her eyes.

Four, she was totally out of her mind.

The villain simply stared and had the decency to look ill at ease.

"Honey, I told you we had someone coming for dinner."

Yes, and she'd asked if the guest was male or female and he said male. So she figured she'd finish planting the black-eyed Susans and get cleaned up while her dad grilled and conversed with his guest.

"Daaaad," Laurel said threateningly.

He straightened and held up his hands. "Okay. I guess my little joke didn't go over too well."

"Joke?" she shrieked.

"Okay. Okay." He gestured toward the unmoving man. "Laurel, this is Marc Goodson. He worked for me one summer . . . oh, about ten years ago. We've kept in touch a few times through the years. He has a perfectly good explanation about this little misunderstanding."

Now what was she expected to do? Walk up and offer a dirty-gloved hand to him? Go up there looking like a wet dog? And smelling worse? After all, she did use fertilizer when planting.

Deciding to let him take the initiative, Laurel knelt and took a plant out of a pot near her. He was walking across the deck when she set the flowers in the hole and lifted them again to put in more topsoil and a little phosphorus.

When he walked down the slope to where she knelt, her heart pounded as it had on the night he'd frightened her.

She felt frightened now — when he stooped down and knelt close to her.

She knew her dad wouldn't have brought him here if he didn't have complete trust in this man. To trust him or not wasn't what frightened her. The problem was, when Marc Goodson softly said, "I'm sorry I've caused you any concern," his voice had the quality that brought back the memory of when she was thirteen years old, with a crush on an older man.

Yes, this was her carpenter.

"I need —" She needed to put things in perspective. "I need to plant the Susans and then get cleaned up. I'm a mess."

CHAPTER 7

A mess?

Marc already knew that Laurel Jones was a very attractive woman. And he couldn't imagine a more adorable one than when she'd fallen back on the yard, gazing at the pot of yellow flowers rolling down the hill as if it were a catastrophe. He'd wanted to run and pick her up and brush the dirt off and tell her not to think badly of him.

As she brushed the dirt off herself, he hobbled to retrieve the pot. She thanked him and snatched it from his outstretched hand. Not once had she asked about his foot, but she examined the plant as if it were some injured child. He could readily see what took precedence.

After apologizing, rather than make a nuisance of himself, he walked back up onto the deck where Harlan was putting steaks on the grill.

The two of them talked while Laurel

planted the Susans, picked up her empty pots and tools, and disappeared down around the corner of the house. About twenty minutes later, she came from the kitchen and out onto the deck. She was wearing denim shorts and a white tank top, both complementary to her tan. Her sun-streaked light brown hair fell freely along her face and down to her shoulders.

He started to rise from the lounge chair where Harlan had insisted he sit and prop up his foot. He was determined to show Laurel he respected her.

"No need to get up," Laurel said.

"At least let me say that I'm sorry we got off on the . . . wrong foot." He cleared his throat. *How stupid can I get?*

She didn't say his apology was accepted. But she did smile before gliding over to her dad and touching his arm. "Want to eat inside or out?"

"Outside," her dad said. "I hope there won't be too many bugs."

Her hands moved to her hips. "I happen to like bugs."

"Great," Harlan quipped. "I'll give you the steak the fly just landed on."

She laughed, so Marc did, too. He'd never given much thought to whether or not he liked bugs. But if Laurel liked bugs, he could learn to like them.

As she headed for the screen door, Marc asked, "Can I help?"

She paused and looked over her shoulder. "No. You need to take care of that" — she grinned — "left foot of yours."

Ah, maybe she hadn't thought his remark too stupid. She did smile before going into the house. Could she mean he had a chance to start over with her?

When everything was ready, they sat at a round table with an umbrella shading them from the evening sun rays. While they ate the steak, salad, and rolls that Harlan took from the grill's warmer, Marc told Laurel about his job at H&H and explained his reason for being out back during the night of the storm.

"I was on my way to explain to you the next day when you . . . when we ran into each other." He hoped she accepted his explanation as valid.

"I'm sorry I misjudged you." She caught her napkin as it threatened to blow away in the sudden breeze. "Should I tell Mr. Banks that I want to withdraw my complaint?"

"No. If anything, he should apologize to you. Edgar could have told you what I was doing outside H&H that night."

"Why didn't he?" She looked at him curiously, lifted her tea glass, and took a sip.

"He didn't want to say anything that might hamper my investigation. If he had told you, then you might have relayed that information to someone in your department, who could in turn tell someone else, and before long all the employees would think they were under suspicion."

"Oh." Laurel set down her tea glass. "I'm beginning to get it." Her eyes widened. "Instead of you being a thief as I suspected — among other things — you thought *I* might be a thief?"

"Well, no . . . I . . ." He got the impression she didn't quite believe him.

Harlan chuckled and said he needed another steak. "Anybody else?"

Laurel said, "No thanks," at the same time as Marc. Then she turned to Marc and continued, "Looking back, I remember that you said, 'Got a lot of plants there, don't you?' — almost like you were accusing me."

"No. You see, I had this mind-set of catching someone that night, and then I encountered . . . you."

She gave him a sideways glance. "Did you check to see if I paid for the plants?"

He was about to lose his appetite. "It's part of my job."

Harlan returned to the table and filled the

ensuing silence. "Laurel, why don't you show him what you do with those plants?"

She didn't answer but instead turned to look at Marc.

About to swallow hard, Marc decided that might be easier to do with a sip of tea. He picked up his glass. He felt as though he was between a rock and a hard place. If he said he wanted to know, she might take that as his admission that he was suspicious of her. If he said he didn't need to know, then he might miss an opportunity to see her again.

After a drink, he set his glass down and said, "I just saw you planting flowers. That's a pretty good indication."

She shook her head. "That's not what I do with them."

Marc nodded. "They're for landscaping where your dad's building houses?"

"I have bought plants for that," she said. "But that's not what these are for. These were looking unhealthy, and I bought them at a reduced price."

"Speaking of landscaping, Laurel," Harlan said, "it's best you don't come around the development where we're building right now. Marc and I are working on a way to catch some of those thieves he's talking about."

Laurel perked up. "I'll be glad to help."

"Sorry," Marc said. "You're an employee at H&H. I can't enlist your help for this. I'd appreciate your not mentioning anything. Just act normal."

"Normal?" Her gaze moved upward for a moment, then she looked at him and smiled. He felt as though a butterfly had gone down his throat and was beating its wings inside his chest.

"Oh, I should have asked," she said. "What happened to your foot?"

He told her about the scuffle at H&H. "It's healing just fine," he added. "I don't have to wear the cast all the time now. The doctor advised me to wear it when I'm at places where the walking might be . . . precarious."

"Ah," Harlan teased. "Today you didn't want to be one of those biblical fools who step in where angels fear to tread, huh?"

"Something like that," Marc said.

Actually, it had been exactly like that. He wouldn't have had to wear the cast to the Joneses' house. But he wanted to appear as the same man who had caused her concern and yet somehow alleviate that concern.

He glanced at Laurel but couldn't tell if she thought his comment was light, serious, or ridiculous. He watched her look at her plate, poke a bite of steak into her mouth, chew, and glance at him with what seemed to be a challenge in her eyes.

Okay, so she wasn't going to make anything easy for him. But that did seem to be a smile on her face after she swallowed and then picked up her glass of tea.

Harlan mentioned he'd like to work out a few details about the plan he and Marc had talked about. Laurel took that as her cue to take their plates into the house and make herself scarce.

After their discussion and not wanting to wear out his welcome, Marc said he needed to go. When he and Harlan reached the front porch, Laurel was kneeling on a tarp, picking dying blooms off colorful pansies in a flower bed.

Harlan thanked him for coming and went back inside. Marc walked down to where Laurel knelt. "I hope everything is cleared up and there are no hard feelings."

"No hard feelings." She stood.

"By the way, what *do* you do with those plants?" He quickly added, "Not because I think you're a thief."

"You're really interested?"

Interested? Is there a double meaning there? "Definitely."

"Are you free in the morning?"

190

In case this wasn't just small talk on her part, he decided on a detailed answer. "My normal hours are 9:00 a.m. to 5:00 p.m. But since I'm my own boss to a great extent and sometimes investigate after hours and weekends, I can take off during the week if I like."

"Then I could use some help with the plants."

"What time should I pick you up?"

"Unless you have a pickup truck or a van, I'll need to take my van."

"I don't," he said.

"Then meet me here. Why not come early enough for breakfast?"

"Oh, you're a cook, too?"

"Nope." She grinned. "But Dad is. Eight o'clock sound okay?"

"Sounds perfect. I'm glad we got to do this, Laurel. Thanks for a nice evening."

"You're welcome." She smiled. "See you in the morning."

He nodded and turned to leave, then stopped. "Oh, any particular way to dress in the morning?"

"Jeans would be fine. Oh, and wear the cast."

Lifting his hand in farewell, he headed toward his car. Her remark must mean that whatever was to occur in the morning would be a precarious situation. But he hoped her invitation meant, too, that with Laurel Jones, he was on the right foot.

Laurel found her dad on the back deck, cleaning the grill. She put her hands on her hips. "That was some little surprise you pulled, Dad."

"Sure was. I hope you didn't hurt yourself when you . . . ahem . . . fell for him." He laughed.

"That is *so* not funny."

His eyebrows moved upward. "Oh? You mean . . . there's something serious going on?"

"Serious? Dad, I've never even talked to him before the night in the storm." Her thoughts went immediately to when she was thirteen and he washed the hurt from her hands. No, she hadn't talked to him then. He had talked and reassured her.

"You talked to him when you ran into him inside the store," her dad reminded her.

"Talk? We didn't talk. He tried, but I stuttered and stammered."

He chuckled. "That's how I felt when I first met your mother — had never been so tongue-tied in my life."

Laurel gasped and laid her hand on the back of a chair. "You've certainly changed your tune from when I first told you about him."

"Well, sure," he said. "That's before I knew who he was."

Laurel hoped her dad didn't realize she was fishing for information when she said, "You told me he used to work for you, but . . . how well do you really know him?"

Laurel went over to the railing and looked down at the black-eyed Susans she'd planted earlier — the place where Marc had knelt down beside her, much as he'd done about ten years ago.

"It's hard to say," her dad began. "You can be around some people for a lifetime and not really know them. With others, it's like instant camaraderie."

Laurel knew the feeling. She turned and faced her dad's profile.

He looked up from the grill and stared ahead as if looking into the past. "Let's see . . . I think it was when Marc had just finished his sophomore year at college. I took him on as a carpenter. He was eager to learn, and I knew there were some family troubles . . ."

"What kind?"

A look of sadness came into her dad's eyes. "I don't need to repeat the details," he said. "But his dad lost his business, then

Marc's mom and dad separated. Marc moved in with his grandmother."

"That must have been hard." Laurel could empathize with anyone whose life was affected by the loss of a loved one, whether by death or a difficult situation.

"Yes," her dad said. "Marc felt the emotional impact of it. I was kind of like a dad to him that summer. He was a good kid. I liked him."

Laurel realized that Marc would have been going through that difficult time when she was thirteen. Yet he'd been kind to her when she hurt her hands. He must have a caring heart. She leaned back against the railing. "So you kept in touch with him through the years?"

Using the wire brush, her dad scrubbed hard at a particular spot on the grill. "He always took the initiative. I wanted him to know I was there for him, but I didn't want him to feel obligated just because I befriended him that summer."

"Why didn't he keep working for you?"

"That wouldn't have been convenient for him. I don't know if I can keep all the facts straight — it's been a long time — but I do know his mom moved to Charlotte. At some point his mom and dad got back together. Marc transferred from UNCA to NC

State." He shrugged. "Through the years there's been a lot going on in his life."

"Like what? Did he ever marry or anything? I mean . . ."

Her dad looked at her and smiled. "No. He never mentioned anything personal like that when he e-mailed me occasionally. He always sent a Christmas card with a brief note about his schooling or a job."

Laurel suspected Marc might have been like a son he would have liked to have. She could imagine the two of them working together on some kind of building project. "Did he ever come to see you?"

Her dad laid down the brush and began to wipe the grill with a cloth. "A few times. Once during his college break and one Christmas when he came to pick up his grandmother and take her to Charlotte."

"But not here?"

"He was here a couple of times. After he found out your mother died, he came and we talked for a long time. Before that, he came at Christmastime. That was the year you went to meet . . . what's-his-name's parents."

"Dad," she chided, "his name is Darren."

He shook his head. "He wasn't right for you."

"I knew that. I told you we were just

friends."

"Well, anyway, I didn't invite Marc here while you were still a teenager. Not after that time when you hurt your hand."

Laurel gasped. "Dad! That was a decade ago. How can you remember something like that?"

He faced her directly then. "When a worker, or any man for that matter, is near my daughter, I don't forget it. Besides," he said more calmly, "I was on the roof and saw what happened. And Marc told me about it. So did you and your mother." He spoke with determination. "I didn't invite him back then because I wasn't about to expose my thirteen-year-old daughter to some twenty-year-old college guy no matter how moral she and he might be."

"Dad, that's silly."

"I knew that. But I couldn't chance anything with my beautiful girl. Besides, your mother thought you took a fancy to him. That's the summer she decided you needed to go to equestrian camp."

Laurel gave a quick laugh. "I wondered how she came up with that. I don't think I'd ever even mentioned anything about riding a horse." She paused. "But I loved it. Anyway" — she shook her finger at him — "now I get the idea you're pushing me toward Marc."

He scoffed. "How did you come up with that?"

"Oh, just a few things." She walked over and sat in a chair at the table. "First, you brought him home. You didn't monopolize the conversation." At that, he gave her a warning glance.

Ignoring that, Laurel continued. "You left us alone out front. You did everything but come right out and invite him to see what I do with my plants."

"Sneaky, aren't I?" He grinned.

"Right. You're no more obvious than the nose on your face."

"Did it work?"

"No." She enjoyed the look of chagrin on his face. If he kept cleaning like that, he'd have the grill shining like a new nickel. "But . . . ," she said, and his head turned toward her. "He did mention he was curious about what I do with the plants."

"Soooo?"

"So . . . since I've decided he's neither a thief nor a stalker, I want to make sure he's not walking the aisles of H&H looking for romance."

Her dad reared back and laughed. "You could do worse."

She huffed. "Well. That's not too high a

recommendation."

"What I mean is, from all I've seen, he has integrity and a great work ethic. I like Marc."

Laurel laughed then. "Dad, I remember the time you didn't like any of the guys I liked, and I didn't like the ones you liked."

"And now?"

Laurel stood and walked over to the screen door. "We'll see," she said noncommittally. "By the way, he's coming in the morning for breakfast. So fix something impressive."

His brow wrinkled. "Well, aren't my pancakes and bacon always impressive?"

She nodded. "As long as I'm not the one who has to cook it, it's impressive."

He dad looked at her and quipped, "Yep, I'd make someone a good wife."

She knew he was kidding, but he had made "someone" a good husband. However, since her mom died, his social life had almost come to a halt. An intriguing thought occurred. She opened the screen door and was ready to jump into the kitchen considering what she was about to say. "Dad . . ." She waited for his full attention. "Have you ever thought about going to H&H, walking the aisles, and bumping into some woman's cart?"

He drew back his arm, threatening to throw the greasy cleaning cloth at her.

"Yiiii!" She yanked the door open and jumped into the kitchen.

Separated by the screen door, they both laughed. Laurel watched him a moment longer as his smile faded and he stared at the grill. How nice it would be if her dad had someone special in his life besides her — or even Marc — to smile about.

CHAPTER 8

Accustomed to rising early, Marc was ready long before 8:00 a.m. Not having to make breakfast gave him extra time to sit at the kitchen table with a cup of coffee and read the *Oak Ridge News.*

Just as he picked up his cup, a front-page headline caught his attention. "What?" The coffee almost sloshed out on the table. The headline read DIFFERING OPINIONS ON FINDING LOVE AT OAK RIDGE'S HOME & HEARTH SUPERSTORE.

Oh no. Would this never stop? Wasn't it enough that the opposing articles appeared in the Asheville papers? Whatever became of customers going to H&H for home improvement supplies?

"I don't think it's good for business," Marc said to Harlan about thirty minutes later when he sat in the Joneses' kitchen while Harlan cooked and Laurel set the table. She looked very attractive in denim shorts and a tank top, her hair pulled back in a ponytail.

But he needed to concentrate on the conversation. The article had been the first subject that came up after Marc arrived.

"How's it bad for business?" Harlan asked.

Seeing Laurel's curious glance, Marc wanted to be careful how he answered. "Not that I have anything against romance," he said. "But newspaper reporters are taking differing opinions. If H&H is asked for the store's opinion, customers may feel they have to take a stand. Then we could lose half our customers. If we say, 'No comment,' we could lose even more."

"Who would be the H&H person to comment?" Laurel asked.

"Probably the manager."

"How does he feel about it?"

"He's all for anything that brings people into the store. But I don't think he sees beyond that." Marc scoffed, "There's even a couple planning a wedding at H&H."

"Now that's interesting," Laurel said. "How do you feel about all that, Marc?"

"That's not the place —" he began and saw her stiffen slightly. Not wanting to be misunderstood, he added. "But like I said, I have nothing against romance."

She gave him a searching look before turning away and taking orange juice from the refrigerator. "Here," he said, standing up and wanting to change what seemed to be a touchy subject with her, "let me do that. If I invite you to my house for dinner, I have a feeling the cooking will be my job." He grinned. "I should say, my pleasure."

He saw Harlan's head turn toward him then. "I mean," Marc said, "when I invite the two of you."

Harlan and Laurel laughed as Marc poured the juice. Harlan set scrambled eggs, pancakes, and bacon on the table. After Harlan asked the blessing, Marc was glad the conversation moved to topics that didn't require an opinion. That is, until the subject of sports came up and they engaged in light banter about who would win the state basketball championship — Carolina or NC State.

After Harlan left for work, Marc walked down to the basement with Laurel. He wanted to make sure he hadn't offended her by his earlier remarks. "I'm not too keen on people intentionally meeting in a store. But," he said emphatically when they reached the bottom of the stairs, "if it happens naturally, then that's fine." She stood still, looking up at him. She no longer reminded him of the child Laurel, but of a beautiful, desirable woman.

Watch it, he warned himself. He'd started to lean closer to her. What happened to his resolve to keep his thoughts and emotions under control? For several years he hadn't wanted to be serious about a woman. As the years passed, he'd accepted the fact that most women his age were married, divorced, or widowed. Why such thoughts anyway? Deliberately looking around at several tables laden with pots of plants, he whistled. "So this is your . . . flower shop?"

She laughed. "Yeah. Over here are some that need pampering. Those are some I'm taking care of until the landscaper can get them planted." She gestured from one table to another. "These are ready for me to put foil and ribbons on, and these," she said, walking over to a table near the garage door, "these are ready to go." A light came into her eyes. "But all this is nothing compared with what I have planned for the future."

"What's that?" He wondered if she had anyone in particular with whom she hoped to share that future. He stood near her, watching as she straightened a bow that was tied around a flowering plant in a pot wrapped in green foil.

He saw the excitement in her eyes when she turned to face him. "I'd like to start my own landscaping business after I finish school. I have one more semester at State. I'm majoring in Horticultural Science and Agricultural Business Management."

Marc thought he understood. "So your interest in plants is what brought you to H&H?"

"One reason," she said. "I wanted a job where I could have a part in supporting myself without letting Dad foot the bills for everything, although he's willing." She shook her head. "It's hard for him to let me grow up. We've depended on each other so much since Mom died. So I also wanted a job doing something I like and to sort of carry on a project my mom started."

"With plants?"

She nodded, setting a plant on silver foil, and with movements as deft as those of a carpenter with a hammer and nails, she brought the green side of the foil up around the plant and asked him to hold it.

While he accommodated, she cut a piece of ribbon from a roll and wrapped it around the foil, just beneath his hands. "Mom used to take fresh flowers or potted plants to people who didn't have any in the hospital where she volunteered," she said while making a bow. "She loved working in her flower beds, and from the time I was little, she and

I would often take cut flowers from her gardens to sick people."

He moved his hands away after she patted the bow and gave the plant a satisfied nod. "So that's why you had all those from H&H?"

She nodded and reached for another plant. They repeated the wrapping process. "When the plants look wilted or have brown spots, the customers don't want them and H&H reduces the price. So instead of chancing their being thrown away, I decided to buy them and treat them, and if they're healthy again, I'll take them where they can be enjoyed."

"To the hospital?"

She shook her head. "Not these. My singles' class from church had a praise and worship time at the Oak Ridge Retirement Center the weekend I returned from college. A few of the patients had no flowers or plants. That's when I decided to bring some."

"Wonderful idea," he said. "I think my church would be interested in a worthwhile project like that. I'm sure there's the same need at other retirement and nursing homes."

Her eyes lit up. "Oh, Marc, that's a great idea. I could write up a note of instruction about each plant, letting the residents know whether they should set a plant in full sun on the windowsill or give them partial sun and how much water is needed. I could even take plant food the residents could share."

Her excitement was catching. "Like a community project," he said. "That would give them another reason to mingle."

"Exactly." Her face glowed with pleasure.

He glanced around the room. "You already have quite an array."

"Yep." She grinned. "But not as many as H&H."

He laughed lightly. "Well, not yet."

She pointed to a stack of plastic trays. "We can put the foil-wrapped plants in these. Each tray holds six. Incidentally," she said, glancing at him, "the plants you saw me loading are on the table near the stairs. These are some I brought home after my second day of working at H&H." She tilted her head in a saucy way. "You didn't catch me loading those, so you might need to hone your security activities."

"Yes, looks like I need to watch you more closely." He knew that wouldn't be difficult.

He saw her smile. But was she smiling about what he said or about the plants on the table?

■ ■ ■ ■

From the moment he stepped through the door of the center, Marc felt as if he was in a different world — a world where older men and women greeted him and Laurel with hugs, smiles, and welcoming words.

He relaxed and particularly liked being called "Laurel's young man." He listened to old men tell a few jokes, and he told a couple of his own.

Laurel looked in on some residents just to say hello and ask about their plants. She and Marc gave plants to new residents. She even exchanged a healthy plant for a puny one in the lobby.

Being in the line of work where he had to be cautious, suspicious, and always on the lookout for criminal activity, he could readily see his need for this kind of positive interaction. And he couldn't think of a more vivacious, cheery person than Laurel Jones to provide it.

"That was one dumb joke you told," Laurel said after she and Marc were back in the van and heading toward the main road.

He placed his hand over his heart. "Mine?"

"Yeah." She lowered her chin and her

voice, trying to mimic him. "What's the definition of a chicken crossing the road?" She shook her head and gave the answer he'd given. "Poultry in motion." She groaned.

"Well, they laughed, didn't they?"

"Yes, because it's so silly."

Marc scoffed. "No sillier than the man who said a boiled egg is hard to beat."

Glancing over at him, she grinned. "You know I'm joking with you."

"Sure. And I've heard the saying that you only joke with people you like."

"Seriously, though —"

"What? You mean that wasn't serious? You don't like me?" Not wanting to risk her giving a negative reply or saying she was involved with someone else, he quickly said, "Now I'm joking."

Her head turned toward him as she executed a turn from the center grounds and drove onto the main road. She gave him a quick glance. He wondered if the bit of color that came into her cheeks meant she was pleased that he implied he joked with her because he liked her.

"They really enjoyed your being there, Marc. I've been told that some of them rarely have visitors. A few never do." Her tone of voice lowered. "And I liked having you there with me. Thank you."

"You're entirely welcome. It was good for me to do things I'd like to do for my grandmother. Of course, I do things for her, but she can't always respond."

"She's . . . ill?"

He nodded. "She's in Asheville at the home for Alzheimer's patients."

Laurel's genuine concern led to his telling about his returning to Oak Ridge a couple of years ago. Bittersweet memories crowded his mind. "My grandmother discovered she was in the first stages of dementia and needed someone to help settle her affairs and be with her for as long as she could stay in her home. I wanted to do whatever I could for her."

"I understand that."

"I know. Your dad said you even dropped out of college to be with your mom."

"I'm glad I did. Even in her last days, she would sit on the deck and watch me take care of the flower beds."

"That sounds nice." After a considerable silence, he spoke again. "Speaking of flower beds, that reminds me. I keep promising myself that I'm going to do something about the weed beds at Grandmother's house." He shrugged. "Frankly, I have no idea how to begin. But I do know she used to like those little pink and white juicy plants. She had them in pots on the front porch. They're long gone now." He scoffed. "I think they probably needed water."

Her glance toward him indicated as much. "That sounds like begonias. And yes, they're succulent plants that need plenty of water. Would you like for me to get a begonia for her?"

"Yes." He liked her suggestion. "Would you like to go with me to give it to her?"

"I'd love to. So do you live in her house or just take care of it?"

"I live in it. It's legally mine since I'm the administrator of her affairs. But to me, it's still Grandmother's house."

"Where is it?"

"In east Oak Ridge."

At the next road, Laurel turned and headed east. "Tell me where."

Laurel had to remind herself to look away from the warmth in his blue eyes. She had her hands full just contending with the morning traffic. She looked straight ahead. *I'm sitting here with . . . my carpenter. And I think he likes me.*

Following his directions, she drove into a residential area of white frame houses and pulled into a driveway. After they were out of the vehicle, she shook her head at the conglomeration of cramped boxwoods and weed-choked bushes. "That is a pitiful excuse for a flower bed."

"Too far gone, huh?"

"Not gone far enough." She waved her hand over it. "Get rid of the whole mess and I'll see what I can do."

"Great. I'll clean the beds out in the evenings and you can plant in the mornings. That way we can work together." When she gave him a quick look, he added, "Separately."

After they drove away from the house, Marc told her he hoped his grandmother could come and see the yard after they finished. "She still has what they call 'a good day' now and then, and they let me bring her home. But those days," he said with a touch of sadness in his voice, "are few and far between. My dad can barely take seeing his mom like that. It's heartbreaking to him and Mom that Grandmother doesn't often recognize them or communicate with them."

"Even if she can't respond, Marc, this can be your tribute to her. It's kind of like my putting flowers on Mom's grave. It's an act of doing something to show that I appreciate what she means to me."

He nodded. "I already feel good about it,

and we haven't even started. But," he said at her quick glance, "I'll start digging today."

Then he made a request she never thought she'd hear from an employee of H&H. "Don't buy the plant from H&H. And it's best if you don't mention our plans to anyone at the store or that your dad is a developer."

"Oh, man" — she turned into the driveway of her house — "I'd love to know what's going on."

"You will — soon, I expect. Be patient."

Patience wasn't exactly her middle name, but soon she felt content sitting on her back porch, drinking coffee, and talking quite personally. She told of having been rather serious about a young man when she was a freshman in college. They drifted apart, however, when so much of Laurel's time was taken up with her mother.

Marc told her about his dad's and mom's problems. Even now, he found it hard to talk about. "They got back together after Dad was released from jail. But my mom just couldn't face the humiliation of continuing to live here." Marc took a deep breath. "Well, I've burdened you with that."

"It's not a burden. I want to know about you, Marc."

He looked thoughtfully at his cup, then

back at her. "I'll tell you this, Laurel. My parents' situation soured me on marriage for a while. Then I was busy trying to find a career where I needed to prove that I wasn't like my dad but was trustworthy. It took awhile for me to realize I didn't need to try to make up for my dad's mistakes." He laughed lightly. "I could make enough of my own."

She smiled at him. He looked beyond her, as if at a memory. "I've dated occasionally, but I wouldn't let myself get serious about anyone."

Laurel wondered if he was saying he still didn't want to be seriously involved with anyone.

"Strange, isn't it," he said. "If that hadn't happened with my parents, then neither your dad nor my grandmother would have played such an important part in my life."

He was beginning to believe in the saying that some good came from the worst of things. He gazed at her. "And you and I probably wouldn't be sitting here —"

He started to reach for her hand, but just then his cell phone chirped, so he reached into his pocket to answer it. "Yes, thanks," he said to the caller, then stood. "I need to go. Business calls."

She stood, too, and he touched her shoulder briefly. He could honestly tell her, "This morning has meant more to me than I can even say."

Yes, Marc. To me, too. But were you trying to say you're glad that we are . . . sitting here together? Or were you warning me that you don't intend to get seriously involved?

CHAPTER 9

On Monday, Laurel used the account of Franklin, her dad's landscaper, at a home improvement store in Asheville for the purchase of bushes. Early on Tuesday, long before the sun would rise high in the sky, she headed to Marc's house.

Marc came out with a cup of coffee for her. She looked up at him from beneath her floppy-brimmed hat, aware of how incredibly handsome he looked dressed for work in a suit and tie.

She took off a glove and reached for the coffee. After a sip, she set the cup beside her water bottle. "You've done a lot of work here," she said. "I don't think you left any of the boxwood roots."

"I tried."

"Thanks." She leaned on her shovel. "This is good dirt."

"Yeah." He grinned. "It looks good streaked across your forehead there."

She wrinkled her nose. "There'll be more dirt on me before I'm finished."

He smiled. "It's your color." His gaze moved to the bushes she'd taken from her van. "What are those bushes?"

"Azaleas," she said. "They're evergreen. And these are nandina. These green leaves will turn deep red during the winter."

He nodded with approval. "Oh, feel free to use the house. When you leave, just lock the door."

She left a couple of hours later, having finished getting the bushes in sooner than she'd expected. His loosening up the soil had made the job easier than if she'd had to dig holes in hard ground.

"It's looking good," he said the following morning when he brought coffee to her. "What's the plan for today?"

"The next rows will be for black-eyed Susans and gaura. Oh, and the gaura is also called whirling butterflies. They look like butterflies when they sway in the wind. These are both perennials."

"Sounds beautiful," he said. "Um, is perennial the same as deciduous?"

"No," she explained. "Deciduous means they lose their leaves. Perennial means the plants either endure from one season to the next or die off during the winter and come back with new growth in the spring."

He smiled. "Perfect. I'll never have to bother with the flower beds again."

"Sorry, that's not how it works," she said. "Somebody will still have to pull the weeds and put down the mulch. And I'm going to plant a few annuals. That means they won't last through the winter."

She finished the work on Thursday and stopped by early on Friday for his reaction to her addition of white polka dot vinca and red salvia.

"Perfect touch," he said. "It's really beautiful." His blue eyes looked into hers for a long moment. "I believe you're a real landscaper."

"Oh, I had to prove it?" She lifted her chin. "When are you going to prove you're a good security agent and catch your crooks?"

"It's up to the police now. We just have to wait."

That intrigued her further, but then he asked if she had receipts for the plants. She retrieved them from her pocket. His close scrutiny and frown made her ask, "Is something wrong?"

"Yes. You didn't include a fee for your labor."

While looking into his eyes, the thought

"labor of love" crossed her mind, but she said, "No charge. I did it for your grandmother."

"Thank you."

His smile and warm blue gaze made her feel rather like a gaura. Before she could whirl, however, he said, "Oh, by the way, one of those newspaper reporters called and wants to interview me. I'm hoping to have time for that by next week. She wants a statement of how I feel about couples finding romance at the store."

"I thought you said they'd probably interview the manager."

"I expected that. But Charlie is married. She wanted to interview a spokesman from the store who is single."

"Well, Marc, what are you going to tell her?"

She thought he'd never answer. Finally, he grinned. "You can read about it in the paper."

That was what her dad said on Sunday afternoon after she returned from having lunch with a couple of friends from her singles' class at church. "It's done. The thieves finally bit."

She sat down, eager to know. "Tell me about it."

"Not yet. The arrest was just made. We

want to make sure this is all done right before it's talked about." He was nodding with a satisfied look on his face. "If all goes well, it should be in tomorrow's paper."

It was — even made the front page. Two young men, Leon "Spike" Riddle and Marvin "Sparky" Cobb, were arrested Sunday morning at a small appliance store in south Asheville. Having been under suspicion by the police, they'd been watched and apprehended after taking new appliances from a new house at Cottonwood Development. Riddle and Cobb were followed by the police and apprehended when they took the items from the truck and took them inside the appliance store. No mention was made of the H&H store.

Her dad explained there had been quite a thieving racket going on with other developers in Oak Ridge and Asheville. "We banded together, and three of us had our builders go to H&H for materials as a ploy to find out if Spike and Sparky had anything to do with it."

"How did the builders set them up?"

"It would be more accurate, Laurel, to say they set themselves up. Marc has known for some time those two fellows have been stealing from the store. And it began to look like an even bigger operation was taking place. We builders legitimately bought materials that we could use, and the police agreed to stake out the developments."

"So this has been going on for a while?"

"Oh yes. But there has to be more than suspicion. There has to be evidence. We builders always report any theft. The police knew they stole from an Asheville house Wednesday night. Friday they went to a development in Skyland and stole lumber. The police wanted to find out if there were several bands of thieves or the same crooks stealing from several different developments. Sunday morning, they stole a washer and dryer, still in the boxes, from my development at Cottonwood."

"On Sunday, of all days. It's like . . . stealing at Christmastime. Somehow that seems worse."

"Exactly, Laurel. But it's what Marc expected. He said broad daylight is a crook's best time to steal. The work sites are deserted. If people do pass by, they're probably on their way to church and don't want to think of anyone stealing on Sunday. If they were seen late at night, then they might be suspected of stealing — but not on Sunday morning."

Marc called that afternoon and gave her a

few more details. "The appliance store where they took your dad's washer and dryer is in south Asheville." She heard his pause. "The store is operated by the brother of your supervisor."

"Mindy?"

"But . . . does that mean she's mixed up in this?"

"I don't have evidence of her being involved directly, but I feel sure she knew what was going on. I try to be careful about judging someone just because a friend or relative is mixed up in something crooked. But I did question her."

"How is she taking all this?"

"She wouldn't talk about it. But that's another reason I'm calling. She quit, Laurel."

"Oh, I hate that. She seemed interested when I talked to her about coming to the singles' class at church. I guess there's no chance now."

"There's always a chance, Laurel. Just as I didn't forget the words of your dad and my grandmother in that difficult time, she won't forget what she should be doing. Maybe she can start over. She does have a good work record here. Which brings me to another point — how would you like to take her place and work days instead of evenings?"

The impact of what was happening with Mindy hit her hard. "I'll have to think about that."

"I understand. Take your time. You have tomorrow off. Think about it. Pray about it."

Laurel had a heaviness in her heart all day. She was glad the crooks were caught. But she felt sad, thinking about how people who had good minds, potential, and opportunity used it in negative instead of positive ways.

She did her laundry and cleaned the bathrooms. Still bothered that evening, she decided to do what she had done many times in the past.

"Hi, Franklin." She walked up to where he was working. "Want some help."

Franklin had taught her a lot about plants, much that she couldn't learn in a classroom. He had to leave early. She told him to take her van and she'd keep the truck. "I'd like to stay and work for a while. If you're going to be here in the morning, I can bring the truck by early enough for you to have the tools."

She worked until long after the sun had set and darkness approached. The recently installed street light shone on the area, allowing her to see well enough to rake out stones and roots until she finally felt tired.

Knowing where the key was for workers who needed to get in when the builder wasn't around, she took that, unlocked the back door, and went inside. She washed up as best she could in the light coming through the small bathroom window.

When she reached for the paper towels, her hand brushed against the key. It dropped with a clinking sound on the tile floor. After drying her hands, she got on all fours and felt around for the key. Just as she started to rise, she heard a step and caught her breath as a bright light shown into her eyes.

"Hey," she yelled. Whoever had the light swung it down out of her eyes and muttered something that sounded like, "What is —"

Blinking away the bright spots before her eyes, she saw a pair of shoes and brought her fists down hard on one of them.

"Owww!" The person stepped back and stumbled away from the door. She heard a louder yelp, a thud, and a couple of grunts as she slammed the door shut. Yes! There was a lock on the bathroom door. The paper towel roll wouldn't make a very good weapon. Maybe she could climb out the window or at least raise it and hope someone would hear.

"Laurel Jones," she heard then, "will you

stop this foolishness and open that door? It's me — Marc."

Laurel felt relief and laughter welling up inside. She made her voice sound serious. "Why did you shine that light in my eyes?"

Sounding close to the door, he answered, "I didn't know you were in there."

"You didn't see the truck?"

"Yes, but I didn't know whose it was."

"So you wanted to shine the light in the truck driver's eyes?"

"Yeah," he said. "I told your dad I'd ride through the development occasionally and keep an eye out for anything that didn't look right. Sometimes kids have been known to go in houses under construction and do some damage. I thought somebody might be in here doing something that shouldn't be done."

She put her face close to the door. "Like . . . using the bathroom?"

"C'mon, Laurel, quit playing games. My foot hurts. I need to sit down."

"There's a floor," she teased.

He moaned, but she unlocked the door.

As soon as she opened it a few feet, his arms came around her waist. "Gotcha." He laughed. "Don't you know better than to open a door to someone you hardly know?"

She looked up into his face. His expression was not at all ominous. But she did feel threatened. A man that good-looking, holding her close, his eyes moving to her lips and then locking with hers, the beating of two hearts together, and his quickness of breath as he stared at her all mingled to make him very dangerous to her — emotionally.

She gave a small nervous laugh and tried to step back. He moved away. She said the only thing — well, not the only thing — but the best thing that came to mind. "Did I really hurt you?"

"That was quite a whack right on the top of my foot."

"Okay, where's the flashlight?"

"In my hand."

She took it and laid it on the cabinet top, where it could shine across the commode and bathtub. "Now sit here."

He gave a short laugh. "I didn't come in here to use the bathroom."

"Keep the lid down. Now sit."

While he sat on the lid, Marc wondered if he should run to protect himself or give in to her whims. He decided to see it through. She lifted his right foot, untied the bow, and loosened the shoelaces.

He helped remove the shoe, then the sock,

and propped his foot on the edge of the tub. Leaning across his leg she turned on the faucet in the tub, tested it, and then had him move his foot under the cool running water.

She sat on the side of the tub and rubbed the top of his foot and then the bottom as gently as if stroking a newborn kitten.

"Someone told me once," she said quietly, "to let water wash away the hurt and take it down the drain."

"That's what my mom used to say to me when I was little."

"I know," she said. "You told me."

"When?"

"About ten years ago at a house you were helping build. I fell and hurt my hands."

"I'd forgotten that." She'd remembered . . . all these years? "I was a college student then."

Laurel nodded. "I thought you were a man."

He smiled. "So did I. But in the past I've known a lot of good men — your dad included — and I've come to realize I'm not half the man he or some others are."

Laurel smiled. "I'm beginning to think being what we ought to be takes a lifetime."

He gazed at her for a long time, wondering if she might be having the same thought as he — a thought he hadn't expected to have — that maybe they might consider that lifetime . . . together?

Someday, he was thinking, *I will tell you that you caressed the right foot, ministered to it. But it was the left foot you struck with your fists.* It hadn't really been hurt. Her fists coming down on his tennis shoes had done no damage whatsoever, even though a bone in that foot had only recently healed.

But he wouldn't tell her for a long, long time. He hoped there might come a day when the two of them would be so close they could almost take each other for granted, when they could say anything to each other.

For now, he wanted to cherish this moment. He'd had many thoughts and emotions concerning this beautiful young woman. He'd wanted to be near her, to know her better, to earn her respect and trust. He'd wanted to hold her, much like he'd held her earlier. When she raised her face to his, he'd wanted to kiss her lips.

But all that, as wonderful as it might be, faded in comparison to what she'd done. She'd loved his foot. She'd caressed his foot. She had a servant's heart. She had a loving nature.

"Does it feel better?" she asked.

"Yes," he whispered and closed his eyes while she turned off the water and gently wiped his foot with a paper towel.

He'd just told himself that a kiss couldn't compare with her so gently touching his foot. However . . .

He stood, and so did she. He leaned toward her, and already her face, lovely in the soft moonlight, was lifting toward his. Somehow, it seemed, his lips had been waiting for this moment all his life.

The kiss did compare . . . quite favorably.

The words Charlie had spoken to him flooded his mind: "Someday you'll get caught."

Marc swallowed hard as he sat and began to pull on his sock, then the shoe. He'd asked, "Who would want to get caught?"

Charlie had said, "Anyone who falls in love."

Marc thought his heart might beat from his chest. Fish got caught, too. And sometimes the fisherman threw the catch back into the river.

Please don't throw me back, Laurel.

CHAPTER 10

Charlie asked Laurel to come into his office after she arrived at work on Tuesday. "I hope you've decided to take the day job," he said. "I'm impressed with your knowledge of plants and the way you connect with customers."

Laurel was sorry things hadn't worked out better with Mindy. She'd had the thought that after she started her landscaping business, Mindy might want to work with her. That wouldn't happen now. And the store did need someone. "Yes, I'll take the day job."

Working with plants and people always lifted her spirits. She loved talking to people about their plants and helping them decide what might be best for landscaping.

She knew her dad had come in to talk with Marc and to thank Charlie and others who had helped with the plan to catch those who had been stealing from houses. Late in the afternoon, her dad stopped in.

"Laurel, you won't believe who I ran into here at H&H." He didn't give her time to ask. "Martha Billings. You know, from church."

"Yes, I know her. What do you mean, Dad? Did your cart run into hers?"

He gave her a warning look. "Nothing like that. At Sunday school we were laughing about what's going on at H&H and that everybody would think the shoppers were looking for a mate. But she said she really needed to replace a bathroom medicine cabinet and asked my opinion. Most women don't know about things like that." He held up a hand. "I know you're not most women. I taught you about carpentry early in your life."

Laurel nodded and tried not to show any expression. But she was thinking that even she could pretend not to know anything about carpentry if it meant getting help from a man in whom she was interested. "So you planned to meet here?"

"No, no. She called and asked if I could today, but I told her I had business to attend to here at H&H and didn't know how long that would take, so I couldn't promise. I told her to go ahead and be looking for a cabinet. I was walking down the aisle, and there she was." His small laugh sounded like a nervous one to Laurel.

"So how'd it go?"

"No problem. We looked at cabinets. She liked my suggestion. I can go over there and whip that cabinet out of the wall and put in the new one. Won't take long." He paused. "You know what she asked me?"

Another rhetorical question?

"She asked if I ever go to the Asheville Bravo Concerts. I told her that I hadn't been since Carolyn died, but I used to enjoy them. She said I should go."

Laurel didn't think this was a time to joke. "Are you going?"

He nodded. "I . . . think I'll help her out. She doesn't like to go to a lot of places alone at night. She's a fairly young widow, and her few single friends don't care for a lot of the concerts. You know . . . opera, symphonies, and such."

Laurel smiled. "Well, Dad, that's nice of you to help her out." Knowing he was staring at her, she tried not to show any emotion that might make him change his mind.

"Um, Laurel . . ." He paused. "Do you suppose you and Marc might like to go with us?"

She smiled then, knowing her dad was ill at ease about going on what looked like a date. "I like that idea."

Laurel's dad invited her, Marc, and Martha out to lunch after church on Sunday to "discuss the issue of the Bravo Concerts," as he put it. "I think it's nice to go out with friends," he said while they ate.

Martha smiled sweetly. "It's always nice to have friends."

Laurel glanced at her and saw the little gleam in the woman's eyes. The two of them shared a secretive smile before Martha picked up her iced tea glass. Friendship was wonderful, but sometimes a friendly relationship could turn into something even more special.

Thinking of that, Laurel addressed Marc. "By the way, that was some article in the paper about you. Let's see . . ." With her elbow on the table, and her fist under her chin, she looked at the ceiling as if trying to remember. Then she looked around at her dad and Martha. "The reporter called him 'a real man' and 'a hunk.' "

"Now you're embarrassing me," Marc said.

"Oh, don't be embarrassed," Martha said. "If I were young enough to talk that way, I'd call you a hunk, too. And I'll admit I've seen some very nice-looking men at that store."

Laurel watched the pink color begin to come into her dad's face. She looked back at Marc. "I was surprised at how positive you were in that newspaper interview."

"Surprised?"

"Yes, you didn't make men and women seem desperate or ugly."

"Right," her dad said. "Marc, I don't necessarily agree with one of your statements, but it caught my attention. You said a woman who knows her way around tools and hardware is irresistible to a man."

Martha spoke up. "I prefer a man who knows those things."

Her dad's face had that pink hue again. "Like I said, I don't necessarily agree."

"Oh," Martha said, "but I was most impressed, Marc, with your saying that all people would like to have someone to love."

"Marc," Laurel said, "were you speaking about the opinion of the store as a whole, or were those your personal opinions?"

"Definitely personal." He gave her a long look.

"When you talked about this before, you didn't seem to approve of couples meeting that way."

"I didn't approve — until recently," he

said. "But after reading the negative remarks one newspaper reporter made, I thought he shouldn't have gone that far. Then, after the paper printed a retraction, I found myself nodding and agreeing. And it wouldn't be good business for H&H if I came off negative."

"Oh, so that's your reason."

"No," he said immediately. "If that were my attitude, I simply wouldn't have allowed the interview. I've come to feel that H&H just might be the best place in the world for couples to meet."

She didn't want to take for granted that he was referring to her. He might be referring to her dad and Martha Billings, so she didn't say, "Me, too."

Laurel was glad she had accepted the day job, which meant she and Marc could see each other in the evenings and on weekends. She'd asked if he'd like to come to the singles' class at her church.

He'd hedged, then given her a quizzical look. "I don't know. Lately I've been thinking about trying out a few couples' classes. I mean, we are a couple, aren't we, Laurel?"

She nodded. "I believe we are."

"I know I'm falling in love with you."

"I've loved you since I was thirteen years

old." Seeing his eyebrows lift, she added, "But I forgot about it for several years. Now it's coming back."

He laughed. "Was that puppy love?"

She shook her head. "If so, would that make what I feel now a mature dog love?"

Although she knew she was in love with Marc, she liked their playful way of talking about it. She had a tendency to be impulsive, which allowed her to appreciate Marc's more cautious characteristics. Her dad said they complemented each other well.

Also, she knew that Marc's allowing himself to become serious about a woman was something new for him.

They visited his grandmother one evening on what the nurse said was "a good day." Although Mrs. Goodson seemed slow in processing things, she knew Marc. He had taken pictures of the flower beds, and his grandmother was delighted to see them.

She loved the begonia. She gave Laurel a long, studied look. "You have a lovely girl here, Marc."

Laurel saw the look of love in his eyes for his grandmother. "I know. I'm glad you approve."

"Oh, I do."

To Laurel, the statement felt like some kind of blessing, coming from Marc's grandmother, who meant so much to him.

The next few weeks were full of activity. Laurel was delighted to learn that the couple who wanted to get married at H&H was an older man and woman. Both had lost their spouses years ago and never expected to marry again until they met in the Garden Shop. Laurel volunteered to arrange plants and trees in a way that would make the event even more special.

"Great idea," Charlie told her. "You fix it up right and I'll call the newspaper reporters. This is going to be great publicity. Oh, and I'll make sure there's cake and punch for all our staff and customers after the ceremony."

She loved talking with Lola, the bride-to-be, about the plans. Lola was as excited as any young bride Laurel had ever seen. "I know this is unconventional," Lola said, "but I feel young and adventurous again and wanted to do this. And we're going to Hawaii for our honeymoon. Ricardo said I could do whatever I want." She tapped Laurel on the shoulder. "Now that's the kind of man every woman should have."

Laurel fell in love with the couple. And on the wedding day in mid-July, the couple stood inside an arbor laced with white flowers on a green vine. Tall trees had been placed on each side of the arbor, and lovely colorful plants enhanced the décor.

Only a few family members were present. Lola said a huge reception was planned, but they'd wanted the wedding to be small. Laurel thought they looked wonderful. Lola wore a light blue dress, and Ricardo wore a dark blue suit.

The staff in the Garden Shop had worn dressier clothes than usual. They took off their smocks in honor of the wedding and stood back from the wedding party as the vows were exchanged.

Laurel stayed near the glass doors between the Garden Shop and main building in case a customer entered and insisted on buying something or wasn't aware of the wedding taking place.

She felt hands on her shoulders, and a voice whispered, "This isn't too bad. Maybe getting married at H&H is all right."

She looked around and up at Marc. "It's very meaningful to them. This is where they met."

He nodded and stepped up beside her. His brow furrowed. "Would you consider getting married in the parking lot . . . by the trees . . . in the rain?"

She stifled a laugh. "I prefer a church."

He nodded and caught her off guard by saying quite seriously, "Have I told you that I love you?"

Her head slowly came around, and she looked up into his blue, blue, loving eyes. He meant it. He'd come right out and said it. "Not exactly that way," she said.

"I want to find a romantic place and tell you that I love you."

"I'll look forward to that."

When the pastor said, "You may kiss the bride," Marc leaned close. "Later," he promised.

She looked over her shoulder at him as he walked back into the store. He glanced back, too, and winked at her.

Her heart beat fast at the anticipation of . . . later.

ABOUT THE AUTHOR

Yvonne Lehman lives in the mountains of western North Carolina, which provides the setting for many of her novels. She is a best-selling author of more than forty books, including mainstream, inspirational romance, mystery, the White Dove series for young adults, and the widely acclaimed *In Shady Groves,* reprinted by Guideposts as *Gomer* in their Women of the Bible series. Yvonne was founder and director of the Blue Ridge Christian Writers Conference for seventeen years until 1993. She now plans and directs the Blue Ridge Mountains Christian Writers Conference for Lifeway/Ridgecrest Conference Center. She is the recipient of numerous awards including the Dwight L. Moody Award for Excellence in Christian Literature, Romantic Times Inspirational Award (first in nation), the National Reader's Choice Award (twice), and first place in the inspirational category of Booksellers' Best Award (judged by booksellers across the nation). She is a member of several groups including ChiLibris; American Christian Fiction Writers; the Faith, Hope, and Love chapter of Romance Writers of America; Mystery Writers of America; and the Writer's View. Yvonne has a master's degree in English (literature) and has taught English, creative writing, and professional and adult studies at Montreat College in Montreat, North Carolina. Visit her Web site at www.yvonnelehman.com.

The employees of Thorndike Press hope you have enjoyed this Large Print book. All our Thorndike, Wheeler, and Kennebec Large Print titles are designed for easy reading, and all our books are made to last. Other Thorndike Press Large Print books are available at your library, through selected bookstores, or directly from us.

For information about titles, please call:
(800) 223-1244

or visit our Web site at:
http://gale.cengage.com/thorndike

To share your comments, please write:
Publisher
Thorndike Press
295 Kennedy Memorial Drive
Waterville, ME 04901